THE GREAT
CZECH NAVY

Books by Richard Katrovas

Green Dragons (1983)
Snug Harbor (1986)
The Public Mirror (1990)
The Book of Complaints (1993)
Prague, USA (1996)
Dithyrambs (1998)
Mystic Pig (2001, 2008)
The Republic of Burma Shave (2001)
Prague Winter (2005)
The Years of Smashing Bricks: An Anecdotal Memoir (2007)
Scorpio Rising: Selected Poems (2011)
Raising Girls in Bohemia: Meditations of an American Father (2014)
Swastika into Lotus (2016)

Edited by Richard Katrovas

Ten Years After the Velvet Revolution: Voices from the Czech Republic

THE GREAT CZECH NAVY

STORIES BY
RICHARD KATROVAS

Carnegie Mellon University Press
Pittsburgh 2018

Acknowledgments

Cabildo Quarterly, Denver Quarterly, Mississippi Review, The Southern Anthology, The San Francisco Review, The Southern California Anthology, Storgy and *Xavier Review*. Several stories also appeared in a chapbook, *Prague, U.S.A.* (Portals Press, New Orleans, 1996).

Special thanks to my brother and erstwhile expatriate Robert Eversz.

Book design by Connie Amoroso

Library of Congress Control Number 2018935071
ISBN 978-0-88748-642-5

10   9   8   7   6   5   4   3   2   1

Dedicated to the memory
of

Alan Levy and Arnošt Lustig

Author's Note

Though the attribution is disputed by some, the late Alan Levy, cantankerous and brilliant founding editor of the *Prague Post,* is credited with proclaiming Prague "the Left Bank of the '90s," and, in some gloriously grotesque sense, it was that. In those first years, trust fund babies, artists and would-be artists, recent graduates fleeing a job-gobbling recession, and thoroughly American-ized Czech émigrés and their Czech-American progeny descended on Prague. The greenback was muscular, though there wasn't yet much to buy, and the Czechs were more or less welcoming. The "expat" community in Prague has gone through several phases that I hope this book accurately reflects, and has more or less blended into a city that has grown more cosmopolitan each year since the Velvet Revolution of 1989.

Most expatriates learn enough Czech to "get around"; very few become anything like fluent. The fact that only ten million people on the planet speak that highly inflected, phonetically difficult and minutely nuanced Slavic lan-guage does not inspire the hard work to learn it. In the early '90s, relatively few Czechs spoke English; now, most folks born around the time of the Velvet Revolution are at least functional in the *lingua franca.* These days, when I deploy my rickety Czech in restaurants, the waiters answer in English. Because my three daughters are fluent in both languages, I seldom have occasion to torture the ears of native speakers.

I shall confess here that my heart roils in nostalgia, atrocious and com-passionate, for '90s Prague, and I can only hope that these stories, a few of which are set as recently as 2013, pay appropriate tribute both to the benignly ignorant Americans who have expatriated to Prague over the past almost three decades, and to the Czechs who have hosted them sometimes bitterly, sometimes warily, but always, in the aggregate, with humor and grace.

Contents

Ann Arbor, Michigan

2004

Data anchored to his very being—address, telephone number, grown children's names and the names of their spouses and small children—suddenly dislodged and drifted over the horizon of phonemic clusters by which they were determined. Sometimes they returned immediately, sometimes well into the night as he shuffled images of intimacy he could no longer name at will. "Sarah," he would whisper, assuring himself he could never forget the name of the woman he lay beside for forty-eight years.

They'd met as kids at school in Ann Arbor, Michigan. Second-generation Greek, she'd lived Greek at home and spoken American English in the rest of post-war Ann Arbor. His first days at school had been the most humiliating of his life; composed of many second-generation Americans, mostly Greeks like Sarah, but also Germans and Irish, the class had laughed as a chorus when it became apparent how little English he understood or spoke. Sarah didn't laugh. She befriended him, taught him. Several years later they were married.

He'd stopped thinking in Czech in his mid-teens, and did not hear the language, except in snippets, for over fifty years. He was American through and through. He cursed and loved and laughed American.

Yet the language of his childhood never left him. He dreamed intermittently in Czech all his adult life, and such dreams were troubling, for in them he was foreign to himself. Since the bouts of forgetting, the Czech dreams had been more frequent, intense, and even frightening. Recently, Nazis had barked on the margins, barely comprehensible as Germans until the vivid dream of three uniformed men dragging his mother and older sister into the other room.

"Sarah," he said to his sleeping wife, shaking her arm gently, "Sarah," he repeated as she rolled slowly, heavily towards him, "I have to go back."

"Okay, darling," she answered, still sleeping.

They arrived on a Saturday in late June. They exited into a storm from the smaller Delta jet they'd transferred to in Frankfurt. There was a bit of rolling thunder and sheets of rain, but not nearly the violence of most summer storms in Midwest America. Jerry Han became Jiří Hanzlík as he stepped into that weather of his early childhood, and descended wet stairs to the slick tarmac.

During the war, his older cousin had taken him to a small town near the Polish border, and from there they had trekked by various painful means to a village near the still smoldering Dresden, through Leipzig, up into Hamburg and from there to Copenhagen, from where they sailed first to Portugal, then New York. Then the bus ride to a thoroughly American, loveless but protecting great aunt in Ann Arbor. After he and Sarah attended the University of Michigan, they took over her family's successful bar and restaurant, Epsilon.

"*Please take us to the Evropa Hotel, through Můstek,*" Jiří stuttered in a language he'd not actually spoken in decades.

"Jerry, I think that's the first time I've heard you speak Czech since we were kids," Sarah beamed. "I'd forgotten how beautiful you sound."

Jiří had indeed avoided occasions requiring that he speak the language. The two or three times he and Sarah had happened upon Czech speakers in Michigan, he'd always made very clear, as subtly though unequivocally as he could, that he did not *speak* Czech. Once, at the restaurant—the entire faculty of the Slavic Studies program at the university were particularly fond of Greek cuisine—a fellow chattered to him in Slovak, and Jerry answered cheerfully and succinctly, but completely in American English. When the young professor asked him, through chuckles and sips of scotch, why he had not answered in Czech, almost identical to Slovak, Jerry responded quite offhandedly that he didn't speak Czech.

"But you understand perfectly!" the Slovak had blurted.

"I didn't say I can't," Jerry had calmly replied, "I just don't."

Nothing and everything seemed familiar on the ride from the airport. The landscape, a bit tamer than what he recalled, a bit thinner, seemed to have retained its subtle hues and delicate geometries. But the garish ads on the side of the highway were from the other world. For a moment, he forgot where he was, and squeezed Sarah's hand, and she knew what he meant. Terror filled him as he gazed upon a Mars Bar ad, the caption in Czech. This was definitely not Ann Arbor, Michigan, and as Sarah gripped his hand and stroked it, he knew with absolute certainty that he was on a road from the Prague airport to the heart of the city of his birth and early years. He relaxed his grip, and so did she, though she continued to stroke his fingers all the way into town.

"*Zastavte!*" Jiří shouted, and the startled driver halted the Škoda cab in the middle of the packed intersection, then slowly, nervously edged to the far curb.

"Jerry?" Sarah said in a low voice as her husband rolled down the window, angled his head out, and gazed up.

"*Mám hlad,*" he breathed to her.

"What?"

"I'm hungry," he repeated.

"What is that building?" she asked.

"*Má maminka, má sestra,*" he answered, then, "*I wanted to help, but the soldiers had guns. . . .*"

"Jerry!" she half shouted, "why are you talking to me in Czech?"

The fear in her voice registered in him, and he reached into his pocket and pulled from it a wad of crowns they'd exchanged for dollars at the airport, and paid the incredulous driver much more than the fare.

The driver rushed to retrieve their luggage from the trunk and push off before the old fellow realized how much money he'd thrown away.

They'd packed lightly for the weeklong stay, and after staring up a long while at the dirty-orange stone building, Jiří dragged the large suitcase by a cord; its tiny wheels squeaked and scraped over the still-damp pavement. Sarah toted the smaller bag with little discomfort.

"I wonder how far we are from the hotel," she said, worried that he had no idea where he was.

"Three blocks straight ahead, then we turn left and go about half a kilometer," he answered, staring off.

"How do you know this?" she asked, considering how young he'd been when he'd left.

"My cousin worked there. I used to take him lunch," he responded, then, with hardly a pause, "*He always shared his food with me. He was like a brother and a father. 'Petře, I would yell up the elevator shaft . . .'*"

"Jerry!" Sarah yelled, putting down the suitcase and grabbing his arm. "I don't understand you!"

"*Proč?*" Jiří answered, perplexed. "I'm not speaking loudly enough?"

"You're speaking Czech, Jerry!"

"What do you mean?"

"Darling, you've been speaking to me in Czech."

Jiří became frightened. This woman who appeared familiar was telling him in English that he'd spoken to her in Czech. What is Czech? He paused to ask her, then said, "Sarah," then again, "yes, Sarah. What did you say?"

"I said let's hurry to the hotel."

"Where's the hotel?"

"Not that far," she answered, gripping his arm with desperate affection. "In the next block we turn left."

"I'm hungry," he announced. He'd not eaten on the planes or in the airports.

"Let's get settled in," she said, "then you can take your medications and we'll eat. What would you like?"

"Dumplings and pork with sauerkraut."

"What is that?"

"What is what?"

"What is that you said in Czech?"

"I think I would like a hamburger," he said.

They checked in and took the elevator to their room, which, upon scanning it, Sarah found adequate. She was bone-weary, having slept little on the L-1011 coming over, and she knew that though he'd kept his eyes shut most of the flight, Jerry, too, had slept little.

"Jerry, let's try to get some shut-eye before we go out, okay? We can eat someplace nice in the evening."

He nodded slowly, wearily, and began undressing, and so did she.

He awoke sweating. The room was not his room. The woman beside him belonged there, but he could not recall why. He splashed water on his face in the dark, ran a washcloth over his skin, and got dressed. He looked in his wallet at his driver's license, and, yes, he was Jerry Han from Ann Arbor, Michigan. He was very hungry. He could read the words on the money, but he didn't know why.

He left the room quietly. In the elevator, he pressed *Přízemí*, and arrived at the lobby. The clock above the front desk said 8:52. It was a little bright outside, so at first he wasn't certain if it was morning or evening, but none of the people in the lobby had morning eyes, and some sat at the small bar off the lobby imbibing.

He was hungry. He was Jerry Han from Ann Arbor, Michigan, and he was married to Sarah, and he was hungry. He wanted a burger.

"Know where I can find a burger, fella?" he asked a young guy by the large sofa in the middle of the lobby.

"Nerozumím," the kid answered, looking away, distracted by a lovely female sitting at the bar. Jerry knew that the kid had said that he didn't understand, but he wasn't sure how he, Jerry Han, knew this.

"*Where can I buy a burger?*" Jerry asked again, and the young guy was visibly startled.

"*There is a McDonald's restaurant on Wenceslas Square,*" the kid replied, and Jiří was happy to hear this, for he recalled once running across the Square with his school mates, Ivan and Jitka, but then Ivan and his family were no longer in the building where they had lived, and Jitka, dear Jitka . . .

He exited the hotel and strode left with an assurance he felt but did not understand, down a street that was not in Ann Arbor, Michigan, into several languages, two of which he understood, and among the people casually chattering them to one another as Jiří passed through and around pairs and small groups on the busy evening sidewalk.

On the Square, two gypsy men asked Jiří in English if he wanted to change money.

"*No Thanks. Where's McDonald's?*"

One of them pointed behind Jiří to a small sign that was a field of red on which was emblazoned a yellow "M." The gypsies scuffed away, and Jerry walked toward the sign.

This was McDonald's. He and Sarah drove through McDonald's after U of M football games. Where was Sarah? Who had won the game? Whom had the Wolverines played? These people did not look like folks in Ann Arbor, Michigan. He stared at the large menu spread the length of the service area, over the heads of the workers, all fair-skinned, and he saw that everything was written in Czech, and he began to sob in terror, and sat down at a table and held his face in his hands and wept for several minutes.

A tall, skinny, pimply boy in a McDonald's uniform, including a paper hat, touched Jiří on the shoulder and asked softly if he was well, and Jiří nodded yes, and said he was very hungry. Then Jerry composed himself, wiped his face with the white handkerchief Sarah always placed in the back pocket of his pants after washing them, and rose.

He stepped up to the counter and ordered a Big Mac, large fries, and a chocolate milkshake.

He ate quickly, and tried to think of nothing but the food before him. Finishing the sandwich, he still had half his fries left, so went back to the counter and ordered a double cheeseburger. He finished this quickly, too, and the fries and shake, and was sad when he was through eating because now he would have to think of other things, things he could not put in his mouth and enjoy.

He walked back onto the Square. It was illumed quite beautifully, especially the National Museum on whose steps he and Jitka played Saturdays in spring. He walked towards the bronze statue of Vaclav on his horse, and recalled celebrating *Mikuláš*, St. Nicholas' Day, when Jitka's father and uncles would dress as the devil, an angel, and Svatý Mikuláš, to roam the evening streets with similarly garbed trios scaring and delighting children. They always finished their cavorting at the statue.

It was dark now, and he would have to go home. He was there in twenty minutes. The courtyard door was locked, which was not right, so he put his shoulder into it and it sprang inward toward the stairs, and he climbed the steps in the dark.

He tried the door; it was locked. He knocked on it, first lightly, then with authority. The door opened, and a woman not his mother or sister stood there in a yellow nightgown. Her skin was very dark, and her hair was long and wavy black. "*Who are you?*" he asked.

"*Are you police?*" she asked.

"*You are gypsy. What are you doing here?*"

"*You must be drunk. What are* you *doing here?*"

Jerry was quite certain that there were no gypsies in Ann Arbor, Michigan, and stared at the dark, hard-featured woman quizzically, who, inexplicably, stared back at him.

"*I ran away,*" he told her. "*I heard them screaming, and I could not bear it, so I ran away.*"

The woman stared at him, expressionless.

"*Father told me I would have to be the man of the house, but I couldn't stop it. I hid behind the big chair by the window.*"

The woman shifted her weight from one foot to the other, placid.

Jerry wondered if Jitka would know what happened to his mother and sister. "*Dobrou noc,*" he said politely to the woman, and climbed one more flight of stairs. He knocked on Jitka's door and stood a long while. He knocked again, and a light snapped on within.

The woman before him was Jitka; certainly it was she. The features of her face, even her hair. "Jitka," he said to his best friend.

"*Who are you, sir?*" the puzzled old woman asked.

"*I am Jiří Hanzlik. Remember? We played on the Square. Our mothers were friends.*"

"*Jiří!*" she exclaimed, and reached across the doorway to grasp his arm, "*I thought you were taken away with the others.*"

"Peter took me to Ann Arbor, Michigan, in America."

"*I don't speak English, Jiří, please . . .*" she said, and sat him down in her small living room, which appeared to Jiří as it always had. The couch was the same. The framed picture of a sailing ship on the wall above the couch was the same.

"I just ate. Have you seen Sarah? She wasn't at McDonald's."

"*Jiří, I said I don't understand English. Please . . .*" she repeated a bit louder, assuming his hearing was a little off.

"*I hid a long time, you know. Until the war was over. I ran to Petr, and he hid me in the basement. He shared his food with me, and then he took me to America. He died, you know. He died quite young in Ann Arbor, Michigan. That is where I live. I live there with Sarah. Have you seen my mother?*"

Jitka was perplexed. It was Jiří. But something was clearly wrong with him. "*Jiří, they were taken to Terezín. It was where many were taken.*"

"I'm an American. I'm an American. I'm an American."

Jitka understood. "*Yes, of course you are an American, Jiří.*"

"I am Jerry Han. I live in Ann Arbor, Michigan. I am married to Sarah. We live in Ann Arbor, Michigan."

"*I think I understand,*" she whispered, and rose.

Jitka played most Saturday mornings with her *banenky*, the cloth dolls her uncle from Munich, through the auspices of the baby Jesus, had gifted her the *Vánoce*, the Christmas of her seventh year. She'd named them Jiří and Jitka, and most Sabbath days played with them in the hall of the ground floor. She sat them at a footstool she adorned with tiny dishes and cups, and when Jiří, his sister Ludmila, and his father and mother passed her and her button-eyed effigies on their way to the synagogue on Jeruzalémská, his father would pause, bow, and greet the dolls and their proprietress.

"*Good day, Jitka! Good day, Jiří! And good day to you, Madam!*" Jiří's father would doff his hat, smiling, before leading his family out the door.

Jiří could see her in the hall mirror; she tapped buttons on a telephone, paused, then spoke hurriedly of an old friend, a boy who is now an old man who has returned for no clear purpose.

Let's Do the Time Warp

Sunday, March 4, 1992

Melissa,

Arrived in Frankfurt an hour late, but made, barely, the Delta hop to Prague. Time-warped and frazzled ("It's just a step to the left. . . ."), I stare out my sooty *okno* onto the gray, snow-dirty *ulice*. The *nebe* is low and dark this late afternoon. I shuffle and look around my little *pokoj*, giving things their Czech names, and try to fix Czech verbs to what things should do or have done to them. Now I speak to you that I may relax into our language a little while, and let you know I'm lonely, tired, a little scared, but okay ("Let's do the Time Warp AGAIN!").

I'd read about this city but never thought I'd see it. I know you think I'm crazy. I am, a little. A broken heart's so boring, so boring anyone so full of love-lost pain she expatriates unto a place like this. May the lying bastard rot in the bliss of his dear wife's arms, may he slowly pass from life cloaked in his renewed affection for her, a fabric interwoven with whatever he feels for the younger mistress who replaced me. Mel, what was I thinking those seven years? Why didn't I listen to you? A fool's lament ("They really drive you insa-a-a-ane!")

Mel, our youths got sucked away. Now we stand upon the planet, sexually intense, attractive and wise with memories of pain and failure, everything good men should want beside them as they enter upon the contingencies and horrors of midlife, but of course we learn that few men are good, and good or bad most will choose, when they may, ingénues in whose compliant smiles no death's heads lurk, in whose caresses are meant no consolations for aging, though the beautiful young are little more than consolation ("In another dimension, / With voyeuristic intention . . .").

Where am I? A Slavic wedge of Europe. At one time the capital of the Holy Roman Empire.

You gave me eighteen months. I've been here fourteen hours and think you gave me too much credit. I flag more from exhaustion than fear of this enchanting, coal-clogged winter city. I've never known a place filled less with threats than sighs, but as I took my first obligatory jet-legged jaunt from Frommer-charmed spot to spot, I felt a dreary, abiding humor apologizing in whispered tones for so much feminine majesty in manly European drag. ("But it's the pelvic thrust . . .")

Mel, you've done Europe. You know how it is. The whole fucking continent, though it pretends plenitude, from city to city speaks a narrow range of nuances within a vast, boring constancy. Jesus Jesus Jesus. Mary Mary Mary. God God God. More than ten billion sold. McChrist on a cross. The Burger King of Kings. Flying Buttresses. Golden Arches. What's the difference? Scale. That's all.

So in the soul department, Europe's got scale. But this place, as European as any scrap of Europe, subverts somehow the fundamental premises of Europe. One has but to stand on the Charles Bridge, best near the middle where I stood, and stare first upon one bank and then the other, allowing eyes to trace the sexy topography, especially how the castle, floodlighted in the late-winter dark like a nightclub torch singer, seems campy medieval testimony to how a treacherous uphill access determines both survival and beauty. The spires are delicate, and delicate the pastel shades which ghost the proper gray of the castle walls, especially when the floodlights first snap on as natural light recedes. Surely, Prague is more woman than Paris, for Paris is outrageously fey, and Prague, whatever her gender, is unself-consciously feminine. ("Well, I was walking down the street / Just having a think / When a snake of a guy / Gave me a wink . . .")

I am not unself-consciously feminine, and indeed grow more self-consciously feminine each year. The price of self-knowledge is metadrag.

This very moment the audible wind became visible with snow. It shimmers in small, quick flurries on the dull air, and a man on the street below just now paused, held out his palm as though receiving change in a transaction with the weather, then turned his coat collar up, stuffed his fists into his big pockets, and pushed on against the deepening evening.

It truly is a remarkable moment when one faces the prospect of living quite alone until death. There are advantages, not the least of which is that when one is exquisitely alone she is less often distracted from the unyielding fact that all of adult life, beyond the securing of necessities and creature comforts, is a condition of waiting for inevitable catastrophes. The disadvantages are few, but irritating, like sand that has gotten into everything, even the food, so that every mouthful is gritty, but not quite so much so that you may not or should not chew and swallow. Sex, the lack of it, is a gritty irritant to the felt passage of time. Chew on that. Feel the grit.

I met a pretty man on the plane coming over. He seemed actually more your type than mine. He was bright and witty besides good-looking, and he took a shine to me from across the aisle. Switching seats with a dyspeptic hen from Houston who grew weary of our chitchat across her enormous, quilted lap, he sparkled with charm. He's a professor of some vague culture-studies stuff; I recall he spoke of demography, he seemed genuinely in love with whatever abstract crap it is he ponders. I feigned mild interest in his life and work and told him as little about myself as decorum would allow. Four hours and nine little whiskies into the exhibition of unvarnished charm, lights went out for the movie and my eyes got droopy. He asked, quite casually, with a tiny whiskey lisp, if I'd like to put my head in his lap. Involuntarily, I glanced down to the place he would have me lay my head, and strapped beneath his pants bulged an arced cylinder of his true intentions. I chuckled, shook my head, cast my gaze away from him toward now-black banks of white clouds far below. He'd worked the airline blanket across his knee, and I'm certain thought that if I'd actually placed my head upon his thigh, he could cover us with a blanket in such a way that . . . Jesus Christ, Mel, has such a man ever persuaded a woman to suck him off in public? Do such things really happen? What kind of woman does such a thing?

So I chuckled—not laughed or merely smiled—I chuckled and looked away and shook my head in what he only could have taken as disgust.

"Forgive me," he half-whispered, deeply and appropriately embarrassed, I thought, until he slipped his card onto my thigh, rose, and took a seat a few aisles back. On the blank side he'd printed the name and number of his Prague hotel.

What kind of man offers a stranger his hard-on for a pillow, then, jilted, actually thinks there's any chance she'll contact *him*? ("It's so dreamy / Oh fantasy free me . . .")

Of course you know where this is leading. I'll meet him in an hour in the lobby of his hotel. He said he'll make a reservation at a place he's heard is very good. Perhaps the offer of his lap had been more chivalrous than I had thought; perhaps I only thought it vulgar subterfuge; perhaps I've only known, for sheer lack of luck, heartless, self-absorbed, woman-hating pricks. Perhaps this one is truly different. Perhaps we'll fuck forever in the lonesome light of Heaven. Oh, Jesus! Oh, God! Oh, boy! Here I go!

Just started the water for my bath. The apartment is steaming up a bit. Checked the thermometer hanging outside the window. Reads minus five degrees. What the hell is that in English? Twenty something? With the wind gusting, this coal-nasty air of winter Prague will make my nipples rap their heels and snap salute. My new coat—got it on sale at Marshall's—is a black and tapered spy-girl kind of number. Continental sexy but fuck-all poor against the cold. Fashion's slave. I suffer, Mel, I suffer!

Just switched on the little black-and-white, poured a glass of Stolichnaya—a liter for three bucks, if I'm calculating right! I soak now in the tub, scratching this in the midst of bubbles I packed instead of good shampoo. One learns a little about one's life when packing for exotic journeys. At thirty-nine, though still an odalisque before the mirror, a woman packs a few such things as offer small and homely comforts, whereas at twenty she likely sailed unknowns solely stocked with vanities.

The TV gushes Czech and though I've studied the language and know a little grammar—four hundred words and eighteen helpful phrases—it is, of course, unequivocally and utterly so strange, jet-lagged as I am, scared, heartbroken and excited. This language seems as strange as men. ("You're spaced out on sensation . . .")

Just now a choir of drunks passed below my window near the bathroom. They howled and cackled, let fly joyous curses, so I guess, upon the cold air, but then, and even as this pen rolls upon the page—now at the main-room table—they set upon John Lennon's "Give Peace a Chance," in English! They are in the fifth round now, each worse than the last, even as each seems sincerer than the last. What a wretched, wretched, sentimental anthem! On Czech news, CNN footage of Sarajevo getting smashed by artillery from surrounding hills, crying babies and wailing mothers and serious Czech voice-over, and on the street below my window a troop of caterwauling Slavs filled to the gills with Slivovice and pilsner slide through the mournful strains of an idiotic

English song imploring peace! Yes, there is a God, and even as He deplores a vacuum, Her predilection in human affairs has been for global camp.

My skin tingles from the hot bath. The smooth cold vodka has warmed the cockles of my heart. What the hell are cockles? Oh, well, they're toasty now, as is this little room.

Bottom line, Mel, is that I've willed a change, a change a step or two beyond my usual self-deceptions. Quitting cigarettes or painting my bedroom or dropping seven pounds or announcing myself celibate at Christmas office parties is hardly sufficient catharsis for spiritual purgation. Nor is trotting off to such a place as this, though at least within the compass of my alien presence among these dour yet funny people I'll achieve, I hope, a measure of reflective calm. That would be nice. And besides, when dreams of romance have been flushed away, when matters of the heart no longer matter, when sex gets hard and nasty for its own salty sake, what else is there?

We'll see how long I last here. I'm sure I'll fall into a working rhythm that will make the place seem like any other for eight or ten hours of every working day. And as Prague sheds her strangeness, as I feel more snug in the passage of time, in the sounds of a language I'll never speak or understand except for elementary transactions, what shall I do and where shall I go?

I scrub my eyeballs and wash the walls of my ears. I compel change without that I may achieve it within. For what and into what I've not a clue, except that it seems clear not to do so would be a petty death and, therefore reeking of cowardice, worse than boring.

I'm off to see the wizard! When this dream winds down, I'll click my ruby pumps three times and swirl back home. Wish me luck, if not in love, then in managing not to step in it. Let's hope these folks curb their passions better than we do.

Prosper, laugh often, write soon. And don't forget to do the Time Warp!

Magenta

King of the Invalids

1993

Jeff wondered why the little guy hated him. Was it just because occasionally he parked Marie's 1994 Škoda Octavia in the marked space in front of the building? During the three months he'd occupied Marie's flat and driven her car, while she lived in his apartment and drove his Chevy Blazer back in Pittsburgh, Jeff had never seen another car parked there, and he pulled into that space only when he knew he'd be in the flat only for a few minutes.

Yet even on those few occasions he'd pulled into the spot, left the engine running and trotted upstairs to grab a sweater or a book, upon returning he'd find yet another note scrawled in Czech and pinned by the passenger side windshield wiper. Though he could make out but a few words, the gist of the notes after the first two seemed implicit in the handwriting; Jeff felt the little man's anger as though it wafted from the ink; a palpable loathing pulsed from the cuneiform-like letters and wing-like diacritics.

Why did that man, King of the Invalids as Marie had irreverently referred to him, cling to his absolute dominion over a parking space that never got used except when briefly pirated by Jeff? And just what was *Svaz Ivalidů*, the organization over which he seemed—by virtue of being the office's lone occupant—to preside?

A Czech colleague from the university informed Jeff that *Svaz Ivalidů* (with an inexplicable tiny "o" over the "u," a diacritic that seemed to make the final vowel even darker) was the Union of Invalids, an organization that dealt with matters of employment, housing, health care, and all other areas of common interest to physically challenged citizens. It was 1993, and there were still such remnants of the old order. His colleague had also translated the first two notes the little man had slipped under the Skoda's windshield wiper.

Note #1:

Sir,

As you are a foreigner, I will assume that you simply do not understand the markings of the sign and on the curb, and continue therefore to park in my organization's space out of forgivable ignorance. I'm certain you will find someone soon to translate this note, and we will no longer have this problem.

Note #2:

Three weeks have passed and you have already entered my space five times. You have had ample opportunity to acquire a translation of my first note, and if you have not it is because you possess a serious flaw in your character. I cannot tolerate further transgression.

Though there had been three weeks between the first and second notes, each time, after the second, Jeff parked in the King of the Invalid's spot he returned to a new missive. This latest was the eleventh, each note a bit longer and exhibiting a more frenetic, more—by Jeff's reckoning—hateful slant than the previous. Indeed, Jeff was even a little frightened to have his colleague translate one of the more recent epistles, and so did not.

Yet, each time he turned the corner onto Rybná and both sides of the block were jammed with the several flavors of Škoda, and there was only that one space in front of his apartment and no other, and he knew it would only take him three and a half minutes to run up, change shirts, check his machine for calls, grab some books and run back down, he would pull into the forbidden space.

Each time, a note.

Jeff stacked them in the desk drawer by the window through which he gazed for hours those days he worked on his chapters, his contribution to a monograph on which he was collaborating with two recently minted Czech PhDs. On a Fulbright, which he combined with a faculty exchange, he'd gotten a pretty good deal, lecturing only one class a week and otherwise using the archives with the help of his English-speaking Czech collaborators, or working alone at the flat. Jeff and his Czech colleagues were seeking to learn how the Party had manipulated demographic data for its own nefarious ends.

He'd spent enough time working at that desk by the window to know that no one ever entered the *Svat Invalidů* office except for its wan ruler who arrived Monday through Saturday at sunrise. And when Jeff passed the office on his way to the vegetable market, or grocery story, or gypsy bar around the corner to have a clay pitcher filled with frothy Pilsner, he would flick a glance through the sooty plate glass and see only the dyspeptic little man behind a bare desk in a bare office. The King of the Invalids would look away and scowl with a wholly regal disdain. Was he plotting disaster? Were there lower limits to his disgust and loathing for one who repeatedly violated his territory?

An auspicious beginning to his academic career had been preceded by an almost disastrous stint in graduate school, where he'd alienated an entire faculty with the exception of his mentor, a strong and brilliant woman who recognized his gifts and trusted time to temper his willfulness. Suffering from multiple sclerosis, she'd chosen him in his second year to be her graduate assistant, a position the duties of which sometimes included helping her from the floor after she'd crossed her braces and tripped, or caught one on a snag in the library carpet and tumbled into a stack of bound periodicals.

His duties also entailed, from time to time, lying down with her, on the carpeted floor of her ample office, and holding her as she wept.

"Jeffy, I think I want to kill myself."

"Doctors say you've got a lot of good years ahead of you. Why would you want to off yourself?" The blinds were closed. Motes shoaled in the meager light that seeped through. He could hear feet scraping between classes, dampened voices.

"Frank finds me disgusting."

"You know, maybe it's not that at all. You're an attractive woman. I think Frank's got issues. I think he may be gay." It was an old joke between them. She was a comely forty-something, and Frank, associate dean of the College of Fine Arts, was twenty-three years her senior. Frank didn't find her disgusting. He was simply past finding her anything but present.

"I'm not just talking about sex, Jeffy. I mean he finds my dying disgusting."

"You've got years, Miriam. Years. You're doing fantastic work. You have an enviable life in so many ways. Please cut the melodrama. You're better than that."

And then he would work his hand up her dress, into her panties, and, slowly, with infinite gentleness, relieve her.

Jeff had grown to love her more than he ever had his own mother, and was devastated in his third year to learn that she'd killed herself. She had overdosed on Oxycodone. He'd felt betrayed. Days earlier, she'd seemed almost joyful.

"Give me a hand, kid. I look like a beached whale!" she'd said, chortling after a fall onto the grass of the Quad, and another time, even as she was going down in line at the cafeteria, "Timber!" He'd hated her for weeks after her death, and buried his hatred, his grief, in the crassest promiscuity. He fucked with a vengeance any female who would have him. He fucked indiscriminately, mechanically though never brutally, until he was numb.

Jeff was certain that conflict is an absolute necessity to psychical, physical and spiritual health, and that those who shrink from it and damn those who don't are the bane of humanity. He believed that any organization that does not encourage good-faith conflict must fail, or succeed at the expense of its members' humanity, which is the ultimate failure. Maximum individuality within maximum community, the young demographer believed, recalling Comte, was the only reasonable goal of humanity. No easy trick, to be sure, but one that, by its very paradoxical nature, centered on conflict.

Physical violence had nothing to do with good-faith conflict as Jeff conceived it; indeed, it was the antithesis of good-faith conflict, for the strongest almost always prevail when violence is an option. Jeff believed that though the lamb may not lie down with the lion, she has the right to try to argue him into a state of docile acceptance of her point of view. More than a decade had passed since Miriam's suicide, and he still could not think except in dialogue with her ghost.

As for his present situation, locked in silent battle with the King of the Invalids, the language barrier made good-faith conflict impossible, and, so, despite the little man's notes (that were probably insane), theirs would have to be a conflict conducted in pantomime. Each time Jeff pulled into the space, if only for a few minutes, he was giving the finger to the hateful little monarch's cruel insistence upon absolute compliance with petty rules; each time a folded page appeared flapping under the Škoda's wiper the little man was biting his thumb at Jeff's situational ethics. Because of the semiotic limitations of such communication, the conflict was more *ad hominem* than Jeff would have liked, yet the regal scowls he received from the king through plate glass suggested that it had indeed become a personal loathing more than a moral position which motivated the notes, and that was precisely the main difference, Jeff concluded, between them: Whereas his position had never strayed from principle, the King of the Invalids, who may have begun with principle as his engine, now coasted down a slippery slope of pure, unadulterated hatred.

The circumstance recalled for him a supremely forgettable, fleeting event from graduate school. Miriam had sent him in her car on an errand; equipped to be operated completely by hand, the C-class Mercedes could also be driven in a standard fashion. At the municipal post office to send a package over night, he'd snaked several times through the packed lot, knowing that the handicap plates on the car assured him legal access to any of the empty handicap spaces. At first flirting with the prospect of pulling into one of the spaces, he'd not been able to bring himself to do so. It would have simply been improper. *He* was not handicapped; Miriam was. It would be petty to take advantage of her single, painfully earned, small social perquisite for his own short-term convenience. Of course, if he'd been driving his Corolla and come upon a packed lot in which there were indeed five or six handicap spaces, well, he'd have had no qualms chancing the retribution of a twenty-dollar ticket, especially given the unlikelihood of a half-dozen handicapped drivers converging, over an eight-minute period, on a municipal post office parking lot. His primary interest was demographics, and Jeff thought largely in terms of statistical reality. In his own car, he'd have occupied one of those spaces without even a twinge of moral doubt.

Miriam had greatly appreciated the release that Jeff from time to time, on the floor of her dark office, would grant her, and tried to reciprocate, though he would not allow her, and simply could not fuck her. She was extremely attractive, yes, his mother's age, but he'd had successful sex with older women numerous times, so his repulsion was not, as far as he could tell, the yucky muck at the end of Freudian attraction. More than a decade later he realized that he'd loved her too much to have sex with her, that he'd been unable, in his twenties, to experience sexual reciprocity with her without having her completely, body and soul. He would have liked to reach back in time and slap that idiot hard on the back of his head.

The king surely knew Jeff was a *cizinec,* a foreigner, probably by noting his name taped to Marie's mailbox. "Jeff Brown" by no feature even approximated a Czech or Slovak name, and, besides, a new Czech acquaintance, a lovely Roma with whom he'd cavorted a couple times a week over the past month, had already informed Jeff that he looked, walked and smelled like an American.

"Americans smile for no reason, walk like they own big ranches, and bathe in vats of fragrant chemicals," she'd joked, and if that depiction exaggerated the Czech image of the American male, it was at least drawn with wary affection. Jeff had learned quickly that if the Czechs harbor few delusions regarding the vagaries of American culture and American swagger, they respected then what they perceived, rightly or wrongly, as a fundamental American decency. And besides, compared to British and (West) German tourists, Americans seemed paragons of social delicacy.

Did the King of the Invalids (Jeff began to place the accent on the second syllable and to flatten the "a" when he thought of his nemesis) hate Americans? Was he an old hard-line commie? Did Jeff strike a figure similar to someone the king had hated when young, some sinister Slovak who'd stolen the heart of a woman the king had loved with an unwavering intensity? Was the little fellow mad? Was an authentic operation actually being coordinated from that spare and tiny street-front office?

Jeff had attended Miriam's on-campus memorial very drunk. He had hit on the chancellor's nineteen-year-old daughter, with a measure of success, though he'd lost interest and never followed up. He'd dressed in paint-splattered jeans and a red tank top that had SPANK THE MONKEY stenciled across the front. He'd drunk Wild Turkey from a silver flask. He'd been asked to say a few words, but upon stumbling to the podium he could barely hold himself steady, and had begun to weep. He'd wanted to shout, "I wish I'd fucked her," but even in such a state had had one censor working. He'd gathered himself, and slurred through a vanilla, three-minute tribute.

In spring, a ghostly bulb quivers awake beneath the earth on which Prague lies, even as above ground the bushes shake off the film of winter coal dust and squeeze forth the colors so painfully absent in the switch-and-stone gray murk of a Central European winter. His conflict with the King of the Invalids had begun in the lap of winter; the first note had stuck to the icy windshield. The last one, the eleventh, had flapped slowly in a sweet spring breeze. The icy sheets over puddles had loosened, broken up, and melted away, but the king's loathing of Jeff hardened into a ragged diamond of disgust. Jeff stared directly into the small man's eyes when passing the office, and though the king averted his gaze, Jeff observed each time the staggering luster of peripheral, hateful regard.

It was on a day when winter shook its bony fist one last time at the Prague sky, shocking new growth and scaring the city's soul back into its subterranean bulb. The cold front was brief but savage; that Monday the temperature had been twelve-degrees Celsius, Tuesday night it was seventeen below zero. For a decade, freakish weather had bothered the planet; that spring in Prague, it excited Jeffery Brown. He didn't know why the cold snap excited him, except that aberrations generally did so. Compelled by his profession to judge reality not by isolated phenomena but by the statistical patterns that events fall into, he lived for anomalies, for nature giving the finger to the normative.

"Reality is the pattern," Miriam had once slurred to him through a martini haze at a faculty party, "but your humanity is the anomalous event regarded, finally, out of context."

Of course, given his fortuitous proximity to a place that reminded him every day of her physical infirmity and therefore of her, since arriving in Prague he'd processed memories of even her sillier cosmic pronouncements with sentimental fondness.

That morning, he took off from work and drove into the countryside. Ice sheeted the road here and there, and drivers were adjusting to the reassertion of winter poorly: cars and a few trucks hugged both white shoulders of the two-lane highway, some negotiating minor accidents, some simply screwing tight their nerves to continue along the treacherous asphalt. Jeff ripped along, happily ignoring the odds that doing so was coaxing misfortune.

"Jeffy, I hope you never know despair."

"Doesn't everyone, eventually?" He'd held her close. It had been late afternoon. Muted light had seeped through the blinds. The hall outside her office had been empty of life.

"No," she'd breathed. They lay in silence for several minutes. "Some go entire, long lifetimes never knowing despair, except in the abstract."

"I find that hard to believe. What do you mean, though, by despair?"

Her quiet weeping had shaded into laughter. "Oh, baby, that you can even ask such a question . . ."

His left shoulder had tingled. He'd moved slightly, assuming a position that would allow blood to flow more easily. A puff of dust, miniscule, had erupted from the carpet as he'd shifted body weight. Her head had been dead weight upon his forearm. "Miriam, you laugh a lot. You love what you do."

"Before the year's done I'll be in a wheelchair."

"Is that so bad?"

A gentle knocking on the opaque glass of her door. Some kid seeking advice, direction, clarification. This had happened often when they lay together on the floor of her office. Eventually, the student had departed. It hadn't been Miriam's office hours, anyway.

"No, it's not so bad, baby boy."

He peeled onto a side road towards a place whose name possessed a honey-eyed cluster of consonants and numerous diacritics, a name that seemed to laugh at its own weird music. He crunched to a halt at a frosted field, got out, and stared at the dust of sparkling crystals over several acres. He had no idea where he was. What did he know about those fields, the people who would plant and tend them? What would he ever know about their difficult, beautiful language in which only ten million people on the entire planet exalted, despaired, wondered, all gathered and propped against one another in the heart of Europe, a space relative to Europe in size as the heart is to the human body?

And what could he ever know of the statistical realities of Communism? So the Party became a Mafia; so the people who were not inside came to loathe those who were; so those who were inside stole from those who were not; so those old enterprises *sans* competition became as men and women without passion, petty and absurd; so the social contract got broken more often than a scoundrel's marriage vows. So what if they became a nation of invalids convalescing in the loveless care of the state. What had been their illness? Inertia, of course. In America, an exotic, powerful strain kills singularly and the bodies get burned. Here, it was as a mild flu that rarely killed, but infected everyone and lingered. But now, a little joy. A little spice. A little romance. The real Bohemian spring had finally arrived.

Note # 11:

Obviously, it is no use. I talk only to myself on this and every page I write to you who cannot comprehend how all waking life is a condition of mourning, neither sweet nor bitter. Who am I to you? A tiny gray man with an absurd role in life. Neither of us, young man, is particularly dangerous. Lacking the courage to do real damage, we merely vex. As I have written to you, and as I shall no doubt write again, that thorny bush across the street has been my point of reference and therefore my salvation. I am indeed a tiny gray man with an absurd role in life, and as I am also old enough to be in mourning my every waking hour, I cannot live day-to-day without a point of reference. Mid-spring, it blooms modestly but sufficiently. Its blossoming is no consolation; the salvation of that bush is not that it bears a fleeting color, for those flowers are but a few seconds of sweetness. The small salvation of that bush is that from my desk, no matter the season, I may gaze upon it. It is mine and it is not mine. It is not a child about whom I must fret. It is only a ragged bush that I needn't tend to, but is there, powerfully present to my eyes, and no one, certainly not one such as you, may with impunity separate me, even for a moment, from my modest salvation.

Meluzína

2007

She first appeared to Sydney Weiskopf on the Charles Bridge in November of 1992. He was in Prague to study Czech brewing methods; his dream was to open a microbrewery back home in Kalamazoo, Michigan. It was 3 a.m.; in several hours he would hop a train to České Budějovice where he would tour the *Pivor Budějovický Budvar*, the Budweiser Budvar Brewery, where a *pivo* infinitely superior to the piss touting the same name in the States is produced. His ethnic German grandfather had been expelled from Bohemia after the war, and had passed down to Syd's father a solemn disdain for Slavic Czechs that dovetailed with nostalgia for a lost homeland. The complexity of such an emotion was lost on Syd, who was far enough removed from Old World enmities to be immune to them.

The woman wore only a large man's white dress shirt that covered her to mid-thigh. Its sleeves were rolled to her elbows. She was barefoot, 5' 4", perhaps, a hundred and ten pounds, fine-featured, not pretty, exactly, but pleasant. Her hair was dark and flowed past her shoulders. There were few others on the bridge, and they were quiet but for a drunken, thick-tongued Slav mid-bridge who sang "Let It Be" a cappella.

Perhaps twenty yards away, the fingertips of her right hand demurely on the south-side stone railing, she stared coolly into his eyes. There was scant light, but enough to see into her eyes from that distance. She smiled, tilted her head, and then leaped over the railing.

He ran to the railing, peered over, but there was nothing, no ripple, no white shirt bobbing to the surface. Sleeping pigeons had not stirred.

As he mimed what he'd witnessed to two somnolent beat cops, he felt like an idiot, and the cops seemed to concur. Shaken, he had no choice but to continue with his schedule, get on with his life.

Each time she appeared, in Prague to which he returned every couple of years, in Kalamazoo where he'd grown up and where he still resided, in Chicago where he often visited, in New York City where he visited about as frequently as he visited Prague, once even in San Diego on a wharf, she leapt out of windows, off of bridges and overpasses, and disappeared.

At his father's funeral, six weeks after his return from that first trip to Prague, as he comforted his mother walking from the gravesite, the young woman appeared in the top branches of a honey locust. It was mid-autumn. She balanced on a high branch amid the forbidding thorns. The tree's pods littered the grass and crunched under their shoes; before he noticed her on high, he was recalling that Indians once made a kind of beer from those pods. Startled at the sight of her, he clutched his tiny mother tightly by her shoulders. The apparition leapt and evaporated. "Was that a dove?" his myopic mother asked.

Now, it is 2007 and he has been in love with the jumper since her third plunge, off the six-story-high roof of the Marlborough Building in downtown Kalamazoo. She'd been peering into the distance as he opened the door onto the roof—towel, book, sunscreen bunched in his arms such that opening the door was tricky—and she turned, gazed deeply into his eyes, and then leaped. The ache of longing at that moment flared, and nothing could soothe it.

Over the years he has called to her, but doing so seems only to hasten her leap. So he remains quiet, savors the moment, her eyes, her smile.

In 1992 he was thirty-four, good-looking, kind of buff. Now he is forty-nine, brews beer but only for his own consumption, and for that of a few friends. He hasn't had a chin since boy Bush's first term, but he is still one of the top two or three sellers at the Subaru dealership. He lives frugally and saves his cash for travel. He spends free time near bodies of water and overpasses, strolling across all manner of bridges. She appears, sometimes, several times a day, sometimes not for days, weeks.

Syd's first wife, when he was in his mid-twenties, left him for a woman. His second accused him of being distant and cold and desired a child that he was unable to give her.

Meluzína, as he named his apparition, has, in her fashion, been as loyal as anyone could hope a lover to be, and she *is* his lover, the sole object of his heart's yearning, the one and only image that triggers his desire.

One day in early spring, cruising home on Stadium Drive from the dealership, Syd notices that the Yummy Dog has closed, and in its place is Psychic Readings. He pulls onto Rambling Road, turns his '96 Lexus around, drives back.

On the tinted plate glass: Marion Summer, psychic. He writes down the website address. At home, he studies the site, makes an appointment.

The Yummy Dog interior of course is gutted of counter, grills, deep fryers, tables and chairs. Mustard yellow is now a deep burgundy. The space is empty but for two overstuffed burgundy chairs facing each other but slightly angled, and a black plastic coffee table hosting a vase of daisies and a fat unlit red candle. A framed mountain landscape hangs above the nook where the main grill sizzled just weeks earlier.

Marion Summer wears jeans and a blue turtleneck. Her dark pageboy is feathered with gray. She is short and stocky, a midlife delivery system for a smile that explodes on her face as Syd enters. She is innocuous, comforting. She gestures toward the chair with its back to the late-day traffic.

She settles into the opposite chair, lights the candle. She closes her eyes, sits back, clutches the chair arms like an astronaut. The candle flares, goes out in the still air; a string of smoke spirals toward the ceiling.

"I can't understand her," she says.

"Excuse me?"

She shifts slightly. Her eyelids flutter. "She's not speaking English. It's not German. Maybe it's Polish, but I don't know."

He'd told her nothing. "Czech. She's speaking Czech."

She opens her eyes. "I can't help you. She's emphatic, but I can't understand. I can't help you."

"If I brought a translator?"

"I can't repeat what she's saying. I can't pronounce the language. She's yelling *po mots* over and over. But everything else seems jumbled."

"She's calling for help. *Pomoc.* It means help."

Syd drives M43 fifty minutes to South Haven. There is a full moon, but the sky is thickly overcast. As he walks the Lake Michigan beach, towards the lights of the pier, he is sorrowful. For almost twenty years she has sought his help across two continents, and he has failed her.

At the end of the pier, behind the extinguished lighthouse, she is standing as he approaches.

"*Prosím, chci ti pomoct,*" he says.

For the first time in fifteen years, as she gazes into his eyes, she steps towards him. Again he says, *Please, I want to help you.*

She takes another step towards him, smiles, then turns and plunges off the pier.

Five skinny boys amble down the pier. They are wearing baseball caps with flat bills, as is the fashion. They fire up a joint, don't see Syd until he emerges from the lighthouse shadow. They glance at him sidelong, warily, but pinch, hit, and pass the dope. Syd would like to join them but knows that he would not be welcome.

Home, Syd packs his one-hitter three times, smokes listening to Dave Brubeck. Crossing lengthwise the archipelago of his time with her, each sighting an island as well as a stepping stone to the next, he lights upon each visitation up to this last, when she took two steps towards him. Years ago he'd begun studying Czech from a textbook and from tapes, but had not thought until tonight to address her in her own language, had not considered that she would not understand his American English. His study of Czech had not gone well, had petered out; he would not be able to communicate with her meaningfully.

He has often wondered if she is always with him, manifesting as she fancies doing so, but only when there is an opportunity to plunge back to that from which she emerges.

"*Prosím, pojď sem,*" he whispers. Then, out loud, "Please, come here." He wonders if he could join her by dying. Hops and yeast overwhelm the pot, permeate the air.

They heard many thundering boots ascending the stairs, and he was certain who had informed on her, that whore's son Fredrick Worl. The SS would torture her for information, and then execute her. He had information to parlay for his life, but not for hers. Wilhelm Weiskopf did not need to speak. They had discussed on numerous occasions what they would do. He wore only trousers, she his white shirt. They climbed onto the radiator, stepped, hand-in-hand, onto the sill of the double casement windows. The parted curtains billowed in the frigid wind. She sobbed once, but made no other sound. He cursed Fredrick Worl, squeezed her hand. A banging at the door became a crash, then another. A growled command then splintered wood and she leaped. He released her hand.

Her terror was not the plunge, but that he'd deserted her. Falling backwards she saw his silhouette disappear from the yellow light. There was only the yellow light.

On his deathbed, floating in and out of lucidity, Tom Weiskopf told his grown son stories of his childhood in Prague. Wisps of German trailed off into Czech then English, and the narratives were incoherent. His father Wilhelm had been a shoemaker, had learned the trade from his father who had learned from his own. The little shop in Prague 5 had been operating continuously for four generations.

Tom Weiskopf was terrified when lucid, telling stories as a stay against the horror of extinction. He described the day the German soldiers paraded into town, how his mother and other ethnic German women threw flowers before them.

"It was a glorious day for Mama and Papa, for all German-speaking Czechs. We felt liberated!"

"You were a child, Dad. How could you have felt that way about the Nazis?"

"They were German. They were of us." The hospice room was cozier than the hospital room had been. There was no television, no radio, just a bed and three hardback chairs. There was a window facing west onto a garden, and in the garden cascaded a miniature stone waterfall. Tom Weiskopf had requested that the window be kept open, despite the chill, so that he could hear falling water.

A sudden breeze moaned through the cracked window, and Tom was aroused from deathward stupor. "Meluzína," he whispered.

"What's that, Dad?"

"It's what the Slavs call the sound of wind in a chimney. "

"Meluzína?"

"He gave up her brothers and their friends, all of them," he said.

"*Opa* did that?"

"They were all executed, but he was allowed to live."

Again, a strong chilly breeze moaned through the cracked window; Syd rose to adjust it, open it a bit more.

"Meluzína," the old man rasped. He slept an hour, heaved several hard breaths, and was gone.

Flesh and blood and ardor, the living woman saw Wilhelm and wife and son on Old Town Square. The cobbler and his family were crossing the square in the direction of the Astronomical Clock. She was accompanying her grandmother on a shopping excursion. The little boy, Tomáš, held his mother's hand and she held her husband's. The tableau of Wilhelm with his family caused a spasm through her body. Her *babi* halted. *"What is wrong, child?"*

Her eyes locked onto Wilhelm's. He looked away. Later, he would swear his love for her. They would make love on the cot in the rear of his shop, the powerful odor of leather an inexplicable comfort to her. When her brothers and their comrades went underground, she served as a courier, shuttling coded messages between cells across the city. Wilhelm pledged his life to her, swore he would die with her. He sent his wife and son to a friend's country home. She moved in with him. He learned everything. Fredrick Worl, his contact in the SS, promised she would be spared.

His days are tedious, his nights intolerable. This December night he pounds back a gallon of his freshest brew. He watches a playoff game for which he has absolutely no interest. On History Channel, a documentary on the influence of the occult on Nazism cannot hold his interest. He takes three tokes of his one-hitter, knocks back another quart.

Past 2 a.m., he stumbles to his car. He cruises Westnedge to Centre and back. The heat is cranked up and the windows are rolled down. A trapdoor opens at the bottom of his heart and everything he's ever cared about that is not she drops out.

Syd has slipped to fourth in sales. His mother is in the throes of dementia. His newest batch of beer is worse than American Budweiser. He has nothing to live for but the occasional presence of a shade. *"Chci jít s tebou,"* he yells.

She stares over the railing of the I-94 overpass. It is 3 a.m.; her white shirt is nearly blinding in his high beams. A small truck grumbles by in the opposite lane. The traffic on the freeway forty feet below is sparse though steady. It is just above freezing and he shivers in his cut-off jean shorts and T-shirt. "*I want to go with you,*" he repeats.

She turns. She does not smile, though her gaze is serene. She reaches towards him.

Or, rather, a snowflake falls upon a leaf. A dog howls. A car door slams. A doe stares into headlights. The wind picks up and moans through barren branches.

Red Ponytail

2008

Ali's father had taken the new job in Prague primarily to get her out of the drug culture of Seattle only to discover that the drug culture of Prague was even more seductive. Homeschooled online, Ali finished her work usually before noon. She was sixteen, and hated that her father had hired a "personal assistant" whose sole task was to keep an eye on her over the hours he was at his job marketing a range of American-made cleaning products. Matilda was only a few years older than Ali, and her English sucked. She watched American sitcoms dubbed into Czech for most of each morning. She was trained as an oral hygienist, but made more money watching TV and ratting on Ali. Matilda was chubby, ugly and mean, and surely resented Ali for her figure, pretty face and Irish Setter red hair.

"Where are you going?"

"Fuck you," Ali answered and shut the door behind her.

"I will call your father immediately!" Matilda shouted down the stairwell.

"What part of 'fuck you' don't you understand, Broom-Hilda?"

On the street, she phoned her dad. "How much are you paying Broom-Hilda?"

"Stop calling her that."

"She's gonna rat me out in a minute for leaving early even though I got my work done; just giving you a heads-up. Get rid of her, Pops."

"I can't leave a minor home alone every day."

"She's a waste of money."

"Where are you going?"

"I'm gonna hang out by the river, feed the swans and ducks, then hook up with Kija when she gets out of school. We'll probably go to the mall."

"Which one?"

"Across the river, the one called Angel, I think."

"Got crowns?"

"Plenty. See you at dinner." She ducked into a little Vietnamese grocery story and bought crackers for the floating birds and a half pint of vodka for herself. She never got carded. As she traipsed down the hill toward the Vltava, she got a text message from her mother, the first since she and her father had arrived in Prague ten months earlier: *How are you, darling?*

Ali snickered and thumbed back: *I'm going down to the river to drink vodka with the birds, and then my friend and I are going to drop acid. Fuck you.*

Her mother had left Ali, Liz, and their father for a colleague, a crackerjack surgeon who'd left his own wife and two young children to be with Ali's mother. Her father had been devastated, but only for a few weeks. A handsome, successful man, he'd brought bimbos from the bars home on weekends, and Ali had had to fall asleep with a pillow over her ear, the other pressed to the sheet.

Ali's older sister Liz had OD'd on heroin just four months after their mother's departure, survived, found Jesus, and thereby was now lost to all. Liz was three years older than Ali, and though they'd never been close, Ali had always admired her older sister's unabashed quirkiness. Even Liz's newly found faith had an eccentric edge to it, seemed gloriously contrived. As long as it worked to keep her from killing herself, Ali was down with it.

I'm always here for you, her mother texted her back. Ali wanted to heave her phone into the river. She wanted to kill something. She threw shards of cracker at the gathering ducks as swans glided toward the free lunch she was offering. She snapped the top off of the little bottle, swigged, grimaced, swigged, grimaced, swigged, grimaced. Her dove-step ringtone startled her. It was her mother.

"How did you get this fucking number?"

"Liz."

"I told her not to give it to you."

"She's living with us now. "

"You're shitting me! That's impossible. Liz would never live in that house!"

"Tell me how you are, about life there. Do you have friends?"

"Oh, Mommy, you know, I'm having loads of fun. Everything is perfect here, just perfect. Is that what you want to hear, Mommy? Do you want to hear that everything is just goddamned perfect?"

"I'd like you to tell me the truth, and to give me a chance to persuade you to stop hating me."

Ali swigged, said through her grimace, "Hate is somehow too bland. Hate is vanilla. What I feel for you is a mixture of butterscotch and dog shit."

"You used to love me so much," her mother said with muted puzzlement, as though they were discussing eye shadow or cheesecake.

"I used to know you, not this monster you became."

After a buzzing, transatlantic silence, Margaret said, "I'm always here for you."

"You never even said you were sorry!" Ali screamed.

"Because I was never sorry, daughter," she replied, and ended the call.

Ali dumped the remaining crackers among the waterfowl; cracker dust at the end of the package glittered in the afternoon sunlight. She finished the bottle and tossed it into the Vltava. She was definitely buzzed, definitely pissed, and definitely wanted to harm something, anything. She stumbled snatching up a stone, almost took a header into the nasty water. She heaved it with all her strength at a mottled swan, struck it in the back at the base of its neck, and gasped at her action as the thing floated away quivering.

Ali filled with remorse, immediately wanted to perform some comforting act, something good, something not full of hurtful rage. She strode unsteadily along the river, shouldering her large cloth bag, feeling a little weepy. When she arrived at the quaint park across the river, she sat among young mothers and grandmothers on benches flanking sandboxes populated mostly by rug rats. Some of the women chattered, some read, one raised her face to the sun with her eyes closed, and seemed to be praying though Ali was fairly certain that she was not; she was maybe thirty, pretty though frumpy in an old and faded plaid housedress. She held her hands in her lap around a sandwich bag of apple slices.

Kija snuck up behind her and covered her eyes. Because this was Kija's standard greeting, Ali didn't even flinch. "You still want a trip?"

"You mean, 'Do you still want to trip,' and yeah, sure."

"It's a trip, right? A noun and a verb. Shouldn't you be able to say it both ways?"

God, this was tedious, unending with Kija. "Look, all I can tell you is when something sounds funny. Using it as a noun in that way just sounds funny."

"But anyone would understand what I meant, correct? You understood."

"Goddamn, girl, just give me the acid." Kija reached inside her shirt and plucked crinkled cellophane from her bra. She placed a tiny, rectangular pill in Ali's palm. "Okay, let's go over this again. Your friends have dropped from this same batch?"

"Dropped what?"

"The acid, dropped the acid? Put it in their pie holes and swallowed it?"

"Yeah, of course."

"And they say they peaked for a couple of hours? It's pretty mellow?"

"Yes, yes, yes," Kija insisted. She was Ali's height but not as developed, as womanly. Since last week, her hair was bleached white with pink accents; her pleated skirt hit her mid-thigh. As usual, she looked ridiculous in a charming kind of way.

Ali pinched the pill and put it in her mouth in one motion. Kija took another one from the cellophane and swallowed it.

"Now let's get the fuck out of here," Ali ordered. "I hate kids."

On the 9 tram, she felt some tingling. As they arrived at the Angel mall, she felt as though someone had plugged a cable *Matrix*-like into the base of her neck and shot current into her. She was fairly certain that no one around her and Kija was aware that they were tripping, but she wasn't absolutely sure that everyone who looked at them—and everyone seemed to be stealing glances—didn't at least have an inkling of their inner states.

As they strode towards the mall entrance, their eyes met, and Kija's grin seemed inappropriate. What was she so happy about? No one's happy on acid. It's not for happiness. It's for being more intensely alive and that's usually some grim shit. "Stop grinning," Ali ordered.

"Why should I? I'm having fun!"

"You call this fun?"

"What is it then?"

"There's no word for it. But it's eight-hundred miles from 'fun'," Ali asserted.

"You are so fucking American!" Kija chucked.

"Should I be offended?" She really wasn't certain if she'd just been insulted.

"By asking the question you make my point."

"You lived there seven years. You're practically one." Kija's mother had taught biology at University of North Carolina-Greensboro, but turned down tenure to return to the Czech Republic.

There was a bookstore to the right of the entrance to the mall. Kija entered it and Ali followed. She definitely didn't want to be apart from her only Czech friend no matter how annoying she now found her.

A dozen or so patrons perused the shelves. Ali recalled that a modest selection of English-language books lay on a table near the rear of the store, by the plate glass window. She eyed Kija's jaunty skimming of bookshelves, her occasional plucking of a book from a shelf for quick close inspection.

On the English-language table were three complete Harry Potter sets; she'd read them all by the time she'd hit puberty, and found the movies a guilty pleasure. There was *Sins of the Mother* by Danielle Steel, a writer her mother called "the biggest hack in all of popular literature." Her mother was very opinionated about books, having published some herself. She'd managed to write novels as a full-time medical doctor, and hardly ever wrote anything about doctors or hospitals. She wrote about women in the late 1800s in California, about how fucked up men were to women back then, much worse even than now.

There was a collection of stories by Philip K. Dick, and Ali remembered a story about electric sheep or something, and that *Minority Report,* starring Tom Cruise whom everyone said is a closeted gay, came from one of Dick's stories. She lifted the book from the table and put it in her bag. A lightning bolt of terror passed through her. She immediately pulled the book from the bag before she could be accused of trying to steal it. She practically trotted to the counter to purchase the book, slapped it lightly on the wood, fished out her wallet. The transaction finished, her hands shaking, she placed the sales slip into the book and dropped the paperback back into her purse.

Ali stared out the window of the bookstore. After-work shoppers were pouring into the mall. No one smiled. No one even acknowledged the humanity of anyone else. It was a Czech thing, and she kind of liked how Czechs were that way, never raising their chins and smiling at strangers, never starting up casual conversations on public transportation, never offering service with a smile. Not only were customers not always right in Prague, they were barely tolerated. This annoyed her father but she loved how waiters and cashiers had such attitude, most of them hating their jobs with a frankness Ali found appealing. They looked so stern, some even sad, as they poured past or into the mall. They looked severe and wise and hilariously weird. As she stood staring, tripping on what she took on faith was LSD, the Czechs moving past the plate glass window, toward or away from the tram stop, from trams into the adjacent KFC or directly toward the mall, they looked like aliens, beings similar to humans but not entirely human; pretty females seemed as though they'd applied make-up with a putty knife. Cute guys looked like they hadn't washed in weeks, and Ali recalled that the only two Czech guys she'd had sex with had stunk of BO; one had been normal size and the other ginormous, but neither had seemed too interested in giving her pleasure, and the big one had been so in love with his dick Ali had told him he should probably marry it, because it certainly did nothing for her but give her discomfort. And both of them had stunk so badly she'd almost gagged. Kija had insisted that it was merely coincidence that Ali had happened to hook up with stinkers, but Ali could tell on trams and in the Metro that many Czechs simply didn't use deodorant.

Kija bought a Czech novel she said was about a young woman hitchhiking all over Czechoslovakia in the early '80s and fucking a lot of really gross truckers. As they left the bookstore and entered the stream of shoppers, Ali saw tracers, like when the Starship Enterprise goes into warp drive, everywhere, and though she had experienced this before, the cacophony of Czech somehow rendered these human tracers more intense, more menacing. And when she saw her mother ascending the escalator in the midst of so many glum Czechs, wearing her white hospital coat, stethoscope hanging from her neck, her long red hair, Ali's own red hair, pulled back into a tight ponytail, she gasped, "Oh my God!" and dug her nails into Kija's arm.

"*Ježíš Maria!*" Kija blurted, "What is wrong with you?"

"My mother's here!"

"You're hallucinating. I just saw my eighth-grade biology teacher from Greensboro."

"Maybe he *is* here."

"He died two years ago."

"Maybe she's here. Her hair is exactly like mine, except long and she wears it in a ponytail when she works."

"I doubt she'd be working in the mall!"

"I've dropped acid more than twenty times. I've never seen shit, only regular stuff all distorted. I saw her clearly." She took Kija's hand and dragged her toward the escalator, not steps but a flat ascending rubber belt. When they arrived at the second floor Ali was frantic. The tracers grew even more intense and she heard music that didn't make sense, polka music played by violins and tubas. The music got louder as she trotted from store to store, peering in and scanning.

"You look crazy. You're making me feel crazy," Kija was staring at her, nose to nose, holding her face hard. "You've got to flow with the flow."

"Go with the flow," Ali corrected.

"You know what the fuck I mean. Flow, goddamnit! Or we'll get busted."

"No one gets busted for drugs in Prague, not for taking them, anyway."

She broke away and resumed her search. But then realized that there was no way her mother would wear her hospital coat and stethoscope into a mall, not back in the States and certainly not here. That Ali was even capable of hallucinating so vividly frightened her deeply, but there was part of her that couldn't let go of that vision of her mother slowly ascending in a crowd, dressed for work. "My sister is living with her and that pig shit our mother is marrying."

Kija was puzzled. She knew that Ali hated her mother, that her mother was a doctor, and that Ali's sister had almost died shooting up too much smack. "That's a bad thing?"

"It's not bad or good. It's just that Liz hated her more than I do. Liz tried to kill herself to hurt Mom." She spotted a white coat, red ponytail. "There she is!" and she took off, but then the image was absorbed into a crowd, disappeared. Still, Ali ran the length of the mall in pursuit.

"I'm leaving, you stupid bitch!" Kija called after her. Ali halted, turned. She was terrified of Kija leaving her. She was terrified of being alone among so many strange people, so many glum aliens. She was terrified of going home and facing her father in her present condition. She was terrified of stinky Czech boys and mindless American ones. She was terrified an asteroid the size of a mall would hit the earth and kill everything. She was terrified of the microbes she inhaled with every breath, the germs she inhaled and blew out. She was terrified that some guy someday might rape and bludgeon her to death. She was terrified of nuclear explosions, nuclear winter. She was terrified that her mother was there, that her mother wasn't there, in a cluster of Czechs at her back, and that her mother, either way, was entirely in her mind.

The Poet

1995

Mid-January, 1994, Margaret had arrived to assume her new post as Cultural Attaché at the U.S. Embassy in Prague. The kitchen Czech she'd learned as a child at her babička's knee in St. Paul had been modified and expanded by a solid year of study, but most of the Czechs she'd met and liked enough to befriend spoke much better English than she Czech. Still, her Czech friends, all well educated and culturally sophisticated, appreciated that she was of Czech descent on her father's side, and that she'd learned to speak at least rudimentary Czech.

She'd known Zuzana and Tomáš for most of the eighteen months she'd lived and worked in Prague, and counted them among the more stable, intelligent and thoughtful people she'd known anywhere. Even as it was obvious that her friendship with them coincided with the slow and graceful disintegration of their marriage, she marveled at their civility, their humble dignity, and how her friendship with them—not with each individually but with them as a couple—developed and deepened in the midst of the breakup.

There were even odd particles of time, usually in the late evenings over wine, when they discussed the dissolution of their marriage as though they were concerned not with their own lives, but with a novel mirroring their lives. How could such honesty be possible? How could they speak so casually and analytically of the end that both acknowledged was now fast approaching, yet remain so equanimous, so intimate?

"I suppose I knew I was falling out of love with Zuzana about the time

I met Marta," Tomáš said on the occasion of what would be Margaret's last visit. Marta was the nineteen-year-old pedicurist with whom Tomáš had had a heartbreaking affair; he'd been so devastated by the beautiful, brainless creature that Zuzana could not help but try to console him.

"He was a mess," Zuzana confided with a sigh to Margaret, and to a strapping embassy Marine named Ned. "He wept himself to sleep for weeks in front of the television, with a glass of brandy in his hand."

"Not every night," Tomáš gently corrected with a wan smile. They'd been through these details on other occasions, but were, in effect, getting Margaret's new companion up to speed.

Staff Sergeant Edward "Ned" Johnson, Jr. stiffened; his crew cut seemed to bristle.

"Look, I've got nothing against guys crying. There are times and places for it. But I'll be straight with you, pal, I don't get it in this case."

"She broke my heart," Tomáš stated matter-of-factly.

Ned leaned forward on the couch. He wasn't much of a wine drinker. He wanted to ask for whiskey. "Well, like, what did she do?"

"She was my passion. Her body was perfect. She was innocent, yet wise about the heart. She fulfilled me."

Ned glanced at Zuzana, who slowly shook her head in odd agreement. "Well, like, didn't it piss you off?" Margaret actually looked forward to the reply.

"Of course I was angry," Zuzana replied, "but his torment was larger than my fury."

Ned liked sex with Margaret. She was twelve years older than he and very alluring, mysterious, and smart. But he hated the socializing. He hated, pretty much, every moment with her except when they were doing it. He particularly hated this. He hated hanging out with these weird Czechs who spoke English better than he did and talked openly and calmly about stuff that should make you want to blow your brains out.

Staff Sergeant Ned Johnson Jr. was not a happy Marine. His father had fought in Nam, three tours; Sergeant Major Edward Johnson had earned the Navy Cross, the Bronze Star and two Purple Hearts. The elder sergeant had definitely been in the shit, and therefore was, as a consequence, a happy Marine still on active duty at Pendleton. Ned Junior had missed the Gulf action, and that dinky Panama thing before it. What was brewing a few hundred miles south in the former Yugoslavia was so fucked up nobody knew who to root for, except that the cowardly bastards doing the "ethnic cleansing" should probably be put up against walls and shot, which Ned figured would probably happen after they'd been allowed to execute more civilians, rape more women.

Ned was a very good noncom who'd missed all the shit, so far. Banging hotsy-totsy foreign-service types was okay fun, but it didn't have much to do with being a trained killer of evil men.

Now this. Why was he listening to this crap? "Margaret, I want to go," he stated, his disgust muted but unadorned. They'd dined on pork knuckle and potato pancakes at a pub an hour ago, quaffed three or four mugs each; he was pleasantly weary, and horny.

"I'm really quite comfortable, and, besides, I'm leaving next month and may not see my friends again."

"Yes, this likely will be the last time," Tomáš added." I've found a flat in Prague 6."

"We're moving him in next Tuesday. My brothers will help with the lifting," Zuzana added.

"Well, congratulations," Margaret said, mildly satisfied that her exit from Prague would coincide with the final untethering of this marriage; it suggested yet another satisfying symmetry in her own life of clean and casual, shallow yet shimmering intimacies.

Ned was pissed. He'd stated his desire nicely. Now what? Sit and listen to more of this? "Look, I've got duty in the morning. I've really got to go."

"Ned, darling, let's finish the wine, then go back to my place, okay?" Margaret patted his knee, then continued to pet it.

Sometimes she treats me like a kid, sometimes like a goddamned dog, he fumed.

"Got some hard stuff?" he blurted.

"I beg your pardon?" Zuzana said.

"Liquor. Got any, like, whiskey, or something like that?" he clarified.

"Of course," Tomáš smiled, rose and wheeled into the kitchen. There was an uncomfortable silence as the three of them awaited his return.

He balanced a black, wooden tray and set it before Ned on the coffee table. It held a small bucket of ice, a tumbler, and a liter bottle of Passport Scotch.

Zuzana and Margaret began to chatter about the problems and virtues of restitution; Tomáš and his two sisters would be restituted this very building. He would allow Zuzana to live in this flat in perpetuity and for free. His new flat would be in a building recently restituted to Zuzana's cousin by marriage on her father's side, and Tomáš would get a great deal. Tomáš listened with an expression of passive goodwill, nodding affirmation of Zuzana's description of their housing reconfiguration.

Ned was a bit taken aback by the formality with which his request had been satisfied. He opened the bottle and poured amber into the tumbler. He needed a chaser. "Can I get a beer out of the fridge?" he asked Tomáš, who nodded, smiling.

Ned fetched a twelve-degree pilsner, popped the top with an opener dangling on a string above the sink. Squatting again on the edge of the couch—all of the furniture in the apartment reminded Ned of his maternal grandmother's house, right out of the '50s—he knocked back three fingers and swigged the good beer. Then he did it again.

Margaret shot a glance at him mid-sentence, but directed no words at him. Zuzana began to describe the towels and linen she'd purchased, for Tomáš's new apartment, at Máj department store, and how much better the store had become since being taken over by Kmart.

Ned poured four fingers and downed it quickly. "You bought his towels?" He slurred a little. "He bangs a hot little number half your age and you buy his fucking sheets? Look, you seem like a nice lady, but that's sick."

A brief silence ensued as the three friends calmly considered this judgment. Ned splashed more cheap scotch into the tumbler, downed it immediately and took a long draw on the beer. A rivulet dripped from his chiseled chin.

"Life isn't necessarily a country-western song," Margaret said. Zuzana and Tomáš smiled and nodded in agreement.

Ned didn't know what she was getting at, but she was definitely putting down country music, and so she was putting down his dead mother, his hero father, and the entire United States of America not including New York City and San Francisco. If they were in a bar, and Margaret were a guy, he'd have to slap her silly. Loretta Lynn would definitely not buy a man's towels after he'd screwed around on her, and then talk about it like the weather. "What d'you mean?" he said finally, swigging directly from the scotch bottle.

"I mean, darling, that men and women aren't necessarily fated to destroy one another's lives and then whine lament."

Ned took a long slug, stood, steadied himself, and walked to the door. "I'm on duty at seven hundred hours," he mumbled. "Thank you for your hospitality." He plucked a two hundred-crown note from his pocket, placed it next to a vase on a table by the door.

"That's not necessary!" Tomáš exclaimed.

Without turning, Ned lifted his left hand to his ear and pushed into the night.

"Sweetie!" Margaret shouted after him.

He turned his head back too quickly, and it made him woozy. "Call me tomorrow, okay?" she said, and tossed his windbreaker at him.

"Yeah," he grunted, and stumbled forward, dragging his light jacket over the pavement, then simply letting it drop. He was too drunk to sleep, and too pissed off. He'd looked forward to bedding down with Margaret, who surely knew that he did not have duty in the morning. Perhaps he'd surprise her later, show up at her door, push in and take her on the couch real rough the way she was always saying she liked it. No, he wouldn't. He was definitely pissed at her, and he wanted her to know it.

The more he thought about it, the more he hated the way she treated him. He needed to hit a good bar, a place where the women were wholesome and horny and the men drank with their heads down, not one of those smoky Czech beer joints where everybody seemed to know everybody and they talked almost as much as they drank.

He'd been stationed in Prague for three and a half months, and had put in for the duty because it was as close as he could get to the shit in Yugoslavia. His executive officer at Pendleton had told him he was being stupid, that working in an embassy was not the route to take for what Ned wanted, but Ned had also simply needed to put some distance between himself and his old man, their shared, wholly unexpressed anguish regarding his mother's death by her own hand and his father's M1911 .45 Caliber sidearm.

As he walked fast and aimlessly, Ned thought about his future, which seemed gray and anything but heroic. He'd probably get out of the Corps and study computers at Fresno State, or join the Fresno police force. He laughed bitterly to himself, realized he'd probably see more shit on the Fresno police force than he will in the Corps.

She'd begged him not to join. She'd begged him to go to college, meet a girl. She'd said it wasn't about a mother's fear for a son's safety. It was about the Corps itself. Her father had been a bird colonel. Her brother had given a leg and a hand to Vietnam. She'd married a man already married to the Corps. She'd said she'd given her own life to the lonely existence of a loyal West Pac Widow. In a moment of utter candor, she'd confessed to both loving and detesting the Corps. She'd witnessed her son being absorbed into the ethos of the Corps, had known that Ned's joining was inevitable. She'd simply wished something else for him. When she'd learned that her breast cancer was stage four and incurable, she'd shown the courage of a warrior. She'd called 911, told the operator precisely what she was about to do and where she would do it. Then she'd put down a plastic tarp on the cement floor of the garage and prostrated herself. As the police had arrived they'd heard the shot.

Ned felt better after he'd puked in a darkened doorway, and stumbled across the bridge one down from the one with all the statues on it. The Charles Bridge was lit up nicely, and the Castle was glazed with a piss-colored sheen. He followed the lights of the street on the other side of the bridge whose name he could not recall, and knew they led to the big square where gypsies and prostitutes, but mostly tourists and cabs hung out, then recalled the little street a couple or three blocks down on the left where, some of the guys had said, the best women were.

When he got there, he didn't see any women, but he heard Johnny Cash echoing from a bar like a loveable old bull; the music gave him a good, warm feeling, so he strode into the bar.

The room was small and not so dirty as trashy, which was fine with Ned. In the center of the far wall was a poster of a droopy-breasted naked woman, below it a small crucifix, and above and to the right a cartoon of a fat soldier drinking beer. As he assumed a stool, Johnny stopped and Tammy started up, and Staff Sergeant Edward "Ned" Johnson Jr. smiled and said the only Czech word he'd ever used, "Pivo," to the bartender. As the chubby, baggy-eyed Slav was drawing his beer, Ned checked out the other animals at the watering hole. A middle-aged couple, shit-faced and silent, leaned into one another at the center of the shabby bar, seeming barely to maintain leverage on their stools, and at the opposite end of the L-shaped bar from Ned sat the ugliest human being he'd ever seen. The troll wore a weird, frozen smile. He listened to the music as though he understood and liked it.

"Oh, Tammy! I love you!" he said in clear English with only the slightest hint of an accent. His voice was rich, clear, and resonant, and seemed not at all to fit the body from which it issued.

"I'll drink to that!" Ned heard himself responding, and raised his glass in brief salute.

"Well, my beautiful boy, are you an aficionado?"

Ned's face soured. "I don't do that kind of stuff, partner. I'm not a fizzy nado, or whatever the hell you folks call it."

The troll paused a moment, mildly perplexed, then clarified, "I'm asking if you like country music."

"Shit yeah," Ned replied weakly, averting his lavender eyes from the creature.

"Country music and bluesy jazz are my favorites!" the troll exclaimed. "If a Billie Holliday and a Merle Haggard were mated, the most American creature imaginable would walk the earth!"

Billie Holiday? Merle had probably gotten a little black tail in his time, but what did that have to do with the fruited plains of America? "Buddy, I don't think of my fellow countrymen as creatures," Ned announced, straightening his spine.

The troll wore a tux; the top button of his ruffled shirt was undone, and a clip-on bowtie dangled from his collar, above which his face glistened in the dull light, as though it were smeared with the grease dripping from the thin, dark hair plastered to his over-size pate; pink moles, most indistinguishable from the pink and purpled zits clustered around them, seemed lit from within by an effervescent puss. The contours of his snout blended into his cheeks such that the two features seemed one. When he smiled, there seemed but the slightest shifting of the general horror, except when through his parted lips black kernels appeared where teeth should have been.

"A patriot!" the troll shouted. "I love that in Americans. I recently read that a poll was conducted in the United States, and then duplicated in most of the countries of Europe. It attempted to measure patriotism. When asked if they were proud to be Germans, only twelve percent answered affirmatively. Such countries as Holland, Sweden, and Denmark placed generally in the low twenties. The Czechs couldn't stop laughing long enough to answer the question. But you Americans! Over ninety percent of you, across the demographic spectrum, answered yes! Yes! Yes! What a blessed wonder to live with such pride in such a world as ours, my friend."

He seemed sincere. "Well, we Americans have a lot to be proud about, mister. I mean, like, I'm a Marine, stationed over at the embassy, and whenever I come on duty and see that big American flag flapping over the embassy garden, I get a lump in my throat. Makes me think of all the Marines who fought and died to keep us free."

"Jaroslav, give this idiot another beer, and a double whiskey on me," the troll told the bartender. "This is so we may toast the United States Marine Corps!" He beamed to Ned as the drinks were set on the bar in front of the handsome young man.

Ned smiled, raised the whiskey to his eyes, "semper fi," he said, and tossed it to the back of his throat and sipped the cold beer.

"Jaroslav, another for the infant," then to Ned, "Iwo Jima!"

"Fuckin' a," Ned breathed, "my granddaddy was there, and one of my great uncles died there."

"The Tet Offensive!"

"My dad was all in that shit," Ned mumbled.

"From Here to Eternity! Patton! Apocalypse Now! Platoon!"

"What?"

"I am John Wayne, Gregory Peck, George C. Scott, Marlon Brando, heroes and antiheroes of the United States Navy, Army, Air Force, and, yes, the Marines!"

"What?" Ned asked again.

"I am Czech voices in many of your greatest war movies!" The troll paused, then, shaping a huge, hideous grin, said, "you see, my beautiful American warrior, I am an actor! And when I am not the disgusting though loveable little monster of a weekly television fairytale, a job for which I wear virtually no makeup, I am the resonant voice of American heroes."

"What?" Ned repeated in a whisper.

"I dub, therefore I am!" the troll chuckled, brandishing his drink in his stubby fingers, sloshing it unconcernedly onto a shiny lapel of his otherwise immaculate black jacket.

"You mean, like when you guys take an American movie or TV show and make 'em talk in your language?" Ned hated turning on *Beverly Hills 90210* and hearing the kids talk to each other in Czech.

"Precisely!" the troll confirmed, then under his breath to the bartender, *"Fill this beautiful goosebrain's glass again, Jaroslav. You would not believe how stupid he is!"* The bartender chuckled softly and shook his head as he filled Ned's glass.

Carrying his glass, the troll slid from his stool and waddled around the bar toward Ned. He managed not to lose his air of dignity as he went up on his toes to place, barely, his glass on the bar edge, and then assumed the stool next to Ned by first jumping up and mounting it on his belly, then working around with comic awkwardness to his fanny. Once settled, he banged on the bar. "Picture it, pretty one," he began, the tiny sausages on the ends of his fat little palms spread before his face, as though the gesture could facilitate the image, "Normandy Invasion! The beach is littered with masses of the dead and dying! You run from the landing craft knee-deep through cold ocean water! Bullets are literally whistling by your ears! Men you've lived with for months, men you've come to love like brothers, are falling dead before your eyes! You hit the beach, drop on your chest and inch yourself and your weapon forward over blood-soaked sand! Then you hear the voice of your commander! He screams, *'Budeme muset přestříhat ten ostnatý drát!'* That's me!"

Ned was dumbfounded. "I don't get it," he blurted.

"What don't you get, beauty? It's a scene from a movie," the troll said.

Ned definitely did not like the bizarre little monster calling him beauty, but what was he going to do, hit him? The troll was simply too weird, too hideously ugly to damage further.

And yet Ned couldn't rise and walk away. His will was fastened to the troll's voice.

"I love America," the troll said wistfully, staring beyond Ned, up and over his shoulder. The troll's voice was so persuasive that Ned could not doubt the sincerity of the sentiment.

"I love the smell of Lake Michigan on a summer night. I love trash compactors. I love cable television and Laundromats. I love the Guggenheim Museum. I love the Golden Gate Bridge, and that desolate stretch of Interstate 10 between San Antonio and El Paso. I love fifteen-year-old girls practicing subliminal seduction in vast suburban malls. I love junior varsity football games. I love the Colonel's original recipe. I love all the bodies on beaches in San Diego. I love O'Hare International in the lap of winter. I love Ted Turner and George Steinbrenner. I love semi-automatic weapons. I love black and whites at Tastee-Freez. I love Christ of the Ozarks and I adore Graceland. Disneyworld is the one true church. I love Jazz Fest in New Orleans and Grand Ole Opry. I love all the mechanisms of sex shops, the ridiculously huge vibrating dildos, especially, and I love Mardi Gras and the Macy's Parade. I love fireworks on the Fourth of July. I love terms like finger bang and Holy Roller and rug rat and well hung and white trash. I love fat bikers who love their own stink, and whose tattoos are the authentic lyric poetry of our age. I love every New World Vampire. I love any hamburger anybody's father grills in the vast American backyard. I love academics who despair their irrelevance. I love Big Business, Old Faithful, and the Washington Monument. I love bathhouses and hospices. I love cardboard boxes so big whole families can live in one. I love especially the obscene, the absolutely obscene sentimentality oozing from every Yankee-doodle farting American I have ever met. I love Long Dong Silvers and his patron saint, Clarence Thomas. I love Richard Nixon and Edward Kennedy and Marla Maples and Barbie and Hugh Heffner's daughter and Billy Carter and Bullwinkle and Dow Jones and Liz Taylor and Alan Greenspan and Dale Evens and Sylvia Plath and every black kid who ever thought, 'shit, I can do that', and became a rap star, and I goddamned adore Art Garfunkel!" The troll drained his glass and banged it lightly on the bar. "*If you understood English, you would not doubt that I am a poet, Jaroslav!* I am a goddamned poet!" He roared in English.

The troll's voice was gargantuan. Ned's spine tingled. He felt so lonely, so far from home. Hank Williams Jr. was singing about the sadness of unfaithful hearts on the radio, and the middle-aged couple, seemingly moving while asleep, rose from their stools and poured out the door like honey. The bartender left his station, probably to take a leak, and Ned felt as though God himself had turned His back on the room. He wanted to rise, turn his back on the demon with the powerful voice, and walk out of the bar, but he didn't know how.

"Want to know why I speak English so well?" the troll asked.

"I don't want to know anything," Ned said, which made the troll chuckle.

"My mother was an American. I got her looks and Dad's brains, but it wouldn't have been much different the other way, believe me! They were both very good mineralogists. She defected in '48 to work for our glorious uranium industry at Jáchymov. Can you believe it? She defected to Czechoslovakia in 1948. Now *there's* a career move!" The troll roared with laughter.

"Please stop talking," Ned begged.

"Calm yourself, pretty one, and finish your drink. It's just you and I now."

"Please stop talking. I don't want to fuck you up," Ned said.

Again the troll snorted with laughter. "It's really remarkable all the hard angles that word has for Americans. Sex, battle, bad luck, dominance and submission. All that in many fine shadings. Nothing like it in Czech."

"Please stop talking."

The troll shushed him with avuncular affection, patted Ned's knee, then began petting it. "I'm your commanding officer in the great Czech navy. I am your superior."

When he was a child, Ned's father had been absent for weeks, months at a time, and Ned had slept with his mother, only to vacate her bed on those rare occasions his father had been home. He'd loved his mother's smell at bedtime. Fresh from a shower, covered in a lotion that smelled of lavender (flowers the color of his eyes, she'd told him), wrapped always in a cotton nightshirt she wore newly washed each day, she read by a small lamp as he breathed her in like a sleeping potion, breathed that clean smell, as clean as angel wings. He dropped his elbows onto the bar and wept into his fists.

"Even your pain is beautiful," the troll whispered, petting his knee. "Go forth, child. I pity you. I pity your beauty."

Dvořak's Fifth

2006

Last night, at an Irish pub off of Old Town Square, Michael beat the shit out of two British skinheads. The Brits were talking at the bar about killing gypsies, and Michael took umbrage. He busted up the little one pretty well, and took down the bigger one and was pounding him when his buddy, Milt, dragged him off and shoved him out the door and pushed him down the alley before the cops arrived.

Milt screamed at Michael, told him what a dickhead he was for fighting in a foreign country. "Why do you always seem to forget we're in a foreign country? You're an idiot. Two assholes mouth off about jacking up gypsies, and you respond violently. What kind of fucking sense does that make?"

Michael knew his buddy was correct, and said so. This morning, his knuckles are sore and his heart contrite. He thinks back on the times, over the past seven months, that Milt has had to extract him from confrontations, save him from himself. The study abroad program he and Milt are attending at Charles University's Faculty of Arts purports to educate motivated American university students in the history, culture, and languages of Central Europe; the reality is that poorly paid, alienated Czech academicians teach in the program to wring a little extra money out of the system, and consequently engage their American charges on intellectual autopilot. One happy consequence of this fraudulent circumstance is that Michael has plenty of time to read books he wishes to read, to imbibe the incredible Czech beer, and get laid.

Michael doesn't seek confrontation. Every conflict he's had in Prague, and indeed every conflict he ever had back in Chicago growing up, was prompted by guys being assholes. If he sees a guy slap a girlfriend, or a couple of big guys picking on a smaller one, or if someone in a bar declares the kind of vile hatred those skinheads spewed last night, a switch trips in Michael; at the core of his being is a fierce need to protect.

He was nine, getting ready for bed, when three men broke open the door of his family's home. One ripped the phone from the wall. Another, a tattoo of a red dragon on the inside of his forearm, lifted Michael by the hair, tied him with a belt around his neck to the banister, and told him if he made any sound they'd kill his sister and mother. The red dragon said that if his sister and mother made any noise he'd kill Michael. Two of them carried knives. Red dragon wielded a baseball bat. They reeked of alcohol. They were all ugly except for the red dragon. He looked kind of like Ben Stiller, but with bad teeth.

Michael's mother, his sister Billie, and he attended family counseling for years. His father left them months after the attack. He sent money, but was otherwise unavailable. He couldn't live with their damages. In some ways, his father's departure was more traumatic than the attack; it certainly got discussed more in therapy.

Michael stopped attending therapy with his mother and sister when he was sixteen, indeed the week he first had sex with Brenda Maxwell. Pressed by Billie as to why he was pulling out of therapy, he confessed that he'd had sex, and that the prospect of spending another hour with her and their mother and Dr. Nancy Brandon now seemed somehow not right. He couldn't say exactly why, but he just couldn't go on.

Billie calls him at least twice a week, always at 4:20 her time, 11:20 p.m. his. It's eight past midnight, and he's puzzled; Billie is brutally habitual. "My battery's low, Sis, how's life?"

"Dad's flown to Valhalla."

From the Legií Bridge, the Castle is beautiful, lit up golden. Czech kids in pairs, German kids in pairs, Italian kids in pairs, American kids in ragged, loose, co-ed gangs saunter from the left bank to the right, stoned or drunk or both. His father overdosed on heart medication. It was definitely not an accident. Billie has no tears in her voice. Recently, she and Michael reengaged with their father, the corporate lawyer who had abandoned them when they'd most needed him. A cool family connection crystalized. He'd not remarried, nor had their mother. There is no mention of a funeral, some kind of memorial. There is no mention of Michael returning to Chicago.

He calls his mother. They chat for a minute and a half. She clearly is not distraught, though there is a tinge of melancholy in her voice, which brightens when the conversation turns to work. She is a world-class chef, owner of the posh Wonder Works on Michigan Avenue. Michael grew up in that kitchen, through high school worked the fish station, assisted the sous chef, learned from his mother. His mother hired a new cook who is very fast and steady, takes instruction well.

"That's good, Mom. My battery's low. I've gotta cut it short. Call me over the weekend, and remember the seven-hour difference."

The night the men assaulted his mother and sister, a cop had to cut the belt from around his neck. Billie and his mother were taken to the hospital; they were able to walk to the medevac unit, though as they passed Michael they did not look at him. They seemed entranced. Four police cars flashed blue light across the walls. Neighbors stood silent, staring. Where was his dad? He always came home before dark, even in winter. It was summer. Tomorrow Michael had a game. He played left field and batted clean up. He was the best hitter on the team. The Blue Socks won most of their games, and he was a big part of the team's success. His whole family was supposed to come to the game. If his father didn't come home, how would Michael get to the game tomorrow? His mother was supposed to wash his uniform.

He was sent to the Bigalow's. Frank Bigalow was in his grade, but a different class. They hung out sometimes, but even though Frank lived across the street and Mr. Bigalow and Michael's father liked to hang together on weekends, sometimes grilling burgers and dogs in their backyards and catching games together, Frank and Michael didn't really click. Frank was quiet. Sleeping in Frank's bed that night was uncomfortable for both boys. Each hugged an edge, back to back. When Michael rose in the middle of the night to pee, he was disoriented.

Michael hops on the 17 tram near the National Theatre and gets off at the stop just after the black-stone tunnel at Vyšehrad. He backtracks and climbs toward the park.

Marta Bozděchová eats an ice cream under a large umbrella covering the picnic-style table at which she sits, on a rise behind the cluster of five-meter-tall statues, two facing north and two facing south across a fifty-meter field. She smiles as Michael approaches and takes a seat opposite. She is very pretty, though dresses a tad frumpy. Michael admires her lack of sartorial self-consciousness. She places her ice cream on its wrapper, extracts from her large, orange plastic purse a pad and pen.

How are you, darling? she writes.

He takes her pen and scribbles, *Já jsem dobrý.*
Mother left for Bratislava today. Would you like to come home with me?
You're not kidding? That would be wonderful!

They've been having sex out of doors because there is little privacy at the dorm, or periods of privacy are unpredictable. Finding nooks far from others' eyes and ears is daunting, particularly because of the noises Marta makes during sex. Deaf from birth, she makes loud animal-like noises during sex, and the noises are constant and varied, like no sounds Michael has ever heard a human being make.

Two of the statues are of Libuše and her peasant husband Přemysl, though Michael can't recall which two, and doesn't much care. The story that Libuše stood on the cliff of Vyšehrad, a hundred meters or so above the Vltava, and presciently saw a great city where there was only water and farmland, makes him think of opera, how the stories are overblown and silly. His father prided himself on being an opera buff. Michael's early childhood was filled with arias wafting from his father's home office. At night, his father sipped whiskey and listened not only to all the great operas, but obscure ones as well. He'd watch any sports event on weekend days, golf, baseball, football, basketball, college and pro; he'd quaff lite beer and stare into the screen, commenting laconically on the competitions. But at night, weekends and weekdays, he swigged Bushmills and rode the strains of operas. Michael hates opera, though is conversant.

Marta looks like a young Diane Keaton, with darker hair and larger breasts, and a tiny mole at the left corner of her mouth. She is fully aware that she looks like Diane Keaton circa *Annie Hall*. She is a student of popular American culture, is fluent in American Sign Language, and reads lips, in Czech and English, quite well, though with Michael she prefers to write. They are very quick in this mode of communication. She is teaching Michael some American signing, though he is not picking it up as quickly as she would like.

They met at the Faculty of Arts, where he is an undergraduate study abroad student and she is in the PhD program in American Studies. She is three years older than he. Her dissertation, the subject of which is still inchoate, will have something to do with the idealization of "silence" in the Deep Image poetry of the '70s, with an emphasis on the work of Robert Bly and James Wright. Michael knows virtually nothing and cares not at all about her scholarly interests, and that is fine with Marta.

We walk she signs. Michael smiles comprehension. They rise. She takes a last bite of her ice cream, vanilla encased in brittle chocolate on a stick, and drops the stick into the trash can flanking the takeout window. She shoulders her gaudy bag and grabs Michael's hand.

Michael loves their utter lack of small talk. Occasionally Marta will point at something, and he'll have to figure out why, though usually her reason for pointing is clear. Otherwise, they walk, holding hands, and Michael can be wholly in his head, with no obligation to feign interest in an interlocutor's observations, commentaries.

As they emerge from the park's second arch, headed toward the first, passing one of the park's relatively well-kept clay tennis courts, they witness a shirtless, clearly drunk or drugged twenty-something, sporting a foot-high orange Mohawk, kick a shivering pit bull.

Marta signs *No no no no no no* over and over.

"Nechte ho!" Michael shouts.

The kid, taller than Michael but slim, his eyes half open, says, "Fuck you." He doesn't sound Czech. He sounds German. The dog shivers, is emaciated; his eyes are gummy, unfocused.

"You kick that dog again and I'll beat the shit out of you," Michael responds, fixing the German punk with a steely glare. Both the guy's nipples are pierced. His nose is pierced in the center, like a bull's. He kicks the dog again.

Marta rips the pad and pen from her purse. *I want to buy the dog,* she writes.

Michael pauses. Glares at the asshole. "We want to buy the dog," he says.

"You want to buy this?" the asshole says; his accent is light, almost regal.

"No, what I want to do is beat you unconscious, you loathsome douche bag. My friend wants to buy it. I'll give you a thousand crowns. It's all I've got on me."

The asshole smiles; most of his teeth are black or missing. "This fine specimen of a beast is worth at least three thousand."

About a hundred and forty bucks. Michael grabs the pad and pen, writes, *I have a thousand crowns. He wants three.*

She writes, *I only have seven hundred.*

"Motherfucker, we have seventeen hundred between us. Take it, or I'll jack you up."

"Adolph and I will wait here while you go to the Bankomat," the asshole says, still smiling.

"No, shithead, you're going to take our money and give us the dog."

Michael presents his palm to Marta. She reaches into her bag, pulls out her wallet, plucks all of the bills from it. Michael takes out his wallet and adds all of the bills in it to Marta's, twelve hundred, not a thousand. He approaches.

He looks into the guy's eyes and sees no fear. The asshole is too fucked up to be scared. Michael kicks him in the nuts. Not hard, just hard enough to make him buckle and fall on his face. Then he kicks him in the ribs. He throws the money on the asshole's back, picks up the leash.

"Dad, what is she singing about?" Michael was eight, in his Superman pj's. It was a Saturday night, so he could stay up and watch *Lion King* for the twentieth or thirtieth time, or read *Harry Potter*, which he was beginning to attempt, with some difficulty. What he wanted was for his father to read the book to him, but his father never read to him. His father lay on the couch in his dark office every weeknight, drinking whiskey and listening to opera.

"The human condition, buddy. She's singing about the human condition." He spoke with his eyes closed. His tie was loosened. His black socks were crossed at the ankles.

"What's that?"

"The circle of life, kind of. And other stuff."

He was listening to Puccini's *Madame Butterfly*, the fifth and final, the "standard" version. Pinkerton had just returned, with his American wife. Butterfly was sleeping, but would soon awaken.

Pinkerton is a cowardly prick, too, Michael thinks. The dog is sleeping on a blanket on Marta's side of the bed. In the distance, a jackhammer is tearing through cement. Marta is sleeping. They are naked. Sex was furious. The dog, Shorty, as Marta immediately referred to him, whined for the duration of their pleasuring one another, though Marta's own vocalizations were fiercer and more varied than ever, contained by walls.

I don't approve of your hurting that boy. But I must confess that I was thrilled in the moment, she wrote after they'd climbed four flights, the dog's nails tat-tatting on the steps.

There is much light in Marta's flat. It is modest, cluttered in an orderly fashion. The couch and two matching chairs form an arc, their floral patterns faded. The dining table, writing desk, china cabinets are dark wood; the piano is nicked up, the ivory keys tinged yellowish. The photos on the walls lining the piano are all of Marta through the years, and of her identical twin sister.

In one—the girls, mid-teens Michael guessed—sat side by side in matching skirts and blouses. Their hair was considerably shorter than Marta's is now.

Michael held the framed photo. Marta fed Shorty scraps, placed down a bowl of water. *Where is your sister?*

She is touring in America. She plays harp in an orchestra.

Michael was fascinated, wanted to know what it was like being deaf and growing up with an identical twin who could hear. But he wanted to have sex, and such a conversation, on Marta's pad, would have been tedious. Now, the late-day sun is blasting through the diaphanous white curtains. Michael's and Marta's clothes are blended in a pile on a dark green, faux-leather chair. Facing away from the window, Marta stirs, reaches behind her to feel for Michael. Finding his thigh, she turns her smiling face to him, her eyes still closed. *Thank you,* she signs. Her eyes flutter open.

"For what?" he mouths slowly.

No go, she signs, and he understands her to be thanking him for not leaving as she slept.

He reaches across her body for the pad and pen. *I'd like to cook for you. I checked out your kitchen, what's in your refrigerator. I want to go buy some things, bring them back and cook you a great dinner. Also, you'll need some dog stuff. I'll hit the Bankomat, then Tesco. Be back in about forty minutes.*

Two plastic bags of dog stuff and groceries on the seat beside him, Michael digs into his pants pocket when the transit agent flashes his badge, and produces his transit pass. The sky is darkening. The 12 tram rattles from stop to stop. A couple of kilometers from Tesco, the car fills, and many riders are standing, holding straps, surfing the tracks, reading. When a humpbacked crone trudges up the steps, a cloth bag in each withered hand, Michael stands, places his bags between his feet, freeing the seats for the woman and her bags.

His parents were in their early forties when he was born, their stellar careers well advanced. Billie, nine years older than he, had been like a third parent, though also a friend and confidant. A corporate lawyer in an eight-year, committed relationship with a woman seventeen years older than she, Billie prodded him to study abroad. She visited Prague four years ago with Malinda, her partner, and pressed Michael to look into study abroad opportunities there, indeed did some initial research into opportunities at Charles University.

His mother retrieved him from the Bigalow's early the next morning. At home, Billie was asleep on the divan in the TV room. His father sat at his desk, his face in his hands. Richard Wagner's *Siegfried* was turned up much too loudly. Michael's mother stormed down the steps, screaming, demanding to know how Michael's father could listen to such proto-Nazi dog shit after what had happened to her and Billie.

At Michael's bar mitzvah, his favorite uncle, Toby, got drunk and declared that if Michael's father showed his face, he'd drag him outside and beat the shit out of him. Michael hadn't yet grown disgusted with his father, held out hope for his return. He wished mightily that his father would not attend so that Uncle Toby wouldn't beat him up. The universe, a power that morphed into his father's cowardice over time, granted his wish.

Wonder Woman, work on your computer and let me cook you something special, he wrote.

He prepares Pork Shashlik with Spicy Red Wine Marinade, one of forty or fifty of his mother's recipes, from her best-selling third book, and a watermelon and squid salad, the recipe picked up somewhere else, though he can't recall the source.

I thought you can't eat pork? she signs, though she has to spell out most of the words very slowly. He signs *Again,* so once again, and even more slowly, she asks about pork.

Michael grabs the pad. The food presentation was as beautiful, as stylish as Michael could make it under the circumstances.

We're quite secular Jews, my mother and sister and I. My father wasn't Jewish. Wasn't? she writes.

He died yesterday. Please eat while the food is hot.

They dined together a few times, in noisy restaurants, usually, and the lack of conversation on those occasions suited Michael just fine. But now, the sound of their cutting and chewing, the sound of forks and knives scraping on porcelain, puts Michael on edge. He grabs the pad. *Does your mother have recordings of your sister playing? I'd like to listen to music as we eat.*

She rises, and fetches a CD. Shorty rouses and follows her. Michael will walk him on the new leash, for a second time, in a few minutes.

Michael loads it in the CD player in the living room. They resume eating the excellent meal. It is Dvořak's Fifth Symphony, very pastoral. Michael can't hear the harp, but it doesn't matter. He just needs noise. Marta is intent on her food. When she looks up, Michael points at her plate, touches his chin, pulling his fingers away quickly, and furrowing his brow: *Is it good?*

Her face brightens within the shadow that slants across the table. She grins. He falls in love with her that moment, and weeps for his father.

Marta writes furiously on her pad, pushes it across the table.

And weeping in the nakedness
Of moonlight and of agony,
His blue eyes lost their bareness
And bore a blossom out to me.
And as I ran to give it back
The apple branches, dripping black,
Trembled across the lunar air
And dropped white petals on his hair.
—James Wright

Michael pours the cheap and hearty Moravian red called Frankovka, topping off their glasses. They finish their meals; the CD player is hissing.

Marta writes: *My father hanged himself. He was dying of cancer. My sister and I found him in the bathroom. We were ten. That's the end of a poem about forgiveness, about forgiving a father.*

He looks up from his plate. Marta stares beyond him, out the window. Shorty whimpers. He is dreaming.

Michael writes, *Was he a good father?*

We adored him. But he knew we would find him. We live with that.

So why?

That question is a wedge between Zuzanka and me. I think, now, that our father's dead body, the sight of it, was a kind of gift.

Michael rises, clears the dishes, tops off their glasses. He will wash and dry the dishes, put them away, and then walk Shorty. *My father was weak.*

A siren erupts blocks away and ceases abruptly. Shorty rouses then drifts off again.

The weak shall inherit the earth.

Meek.

What's the difference? she writes.

I think I love you, he scrawls.

I love I think you! she writes back.

Her laugh, like her lovemaking sounds, is unabashed, unmediated, a perfect expression of happiness, a music that is marrow, a music in the bones.

Red Beans

2013

When Pat received the email asserting that her nineteen-year-old daughter was making porn in Prague, she convulsed for forty minutes as though she'd learned that Missy had died. Then she went online and purchased a ticket from Delta, and booked a room at a hotel called Pyramida.

She cleared her schedule of clients through Thursday of the following week, and called Missy's father. She no longer hated Fred; she wished he were dead for how poorly he'd conducted his relationship with their daughter, but such a wish always has two edges. With the other edge she'd simply slice off his balls.

"Some girl, said she's Missy's roommate, emailed me the news."

Silence. "What can we do?"

"I'm flying over tomorrow morning. I want you to help me pay for the trip."

Silence.

"Fred, fucking man up for once in your life. You make ten times as much as I do. I let you off the motherfucking hook for child support for three years."

"Okay, yeah, Pat. Use the American Express. I'll pay it." They'd kept an American Express account in common for Missy's sake.

"I only want you to pay for half. Did you hear what I said? Our daughter is making porn in the Czech Republic."

"Maybe her roommate is fucking with you. Maybe she's pissed at Missy and this is how she's hurting her."

"Maybe pigs fly in Central Europe. Missy hasn't answered my emails. She doesn't answer her phone."

"You always assume the worst."

"And I'm always right."

She'd assumed that Fred was screwing his business partner, and indeed he had been. She'd assumed that her husband was gay, and he was. She'd assumed that Fred had lied to her, implicitly and explicitly, every day of their marriage, and he had.

Missy adored her father and his partner, Marc. They'd smoked weed with her. They'd encouraged her to explore her sexuality from the time she'd reached puberty. Since she'd spent more time with them in their French Quarter home than with Pat in her uptown shotgun, Fred had argued that he shouldn't have had to pay child support. Pat had argued that, regardless of the fact that Missy had spent so much time with "the boys," as Missy referred to her father and Marc, she, Pat, still had had to maintain all of the practical, quotidian structures necessary to a healthy home life. She'd actually used the phrase "healthy home life," and Fred, Marc, and Missy had cried, "homophobia!"

Pat had tried to explain that many gay couples maintain healthy home lives for children; Fred and Marc were simply not such a couple given their tendency towards weekend debauchery with their gay tribe, festivities that Missy had been planted in the midst of from the time she was eight.

"Yeah, Pat, you're always right. Always."

"Have you been in touch with her?"

"Sure. We exchange emails. She calls almost every Sunday."

"When's the last time you were in touch."

Silence. He was shuffling through memories. "I don't know. It's been a couple of weeks."

"What's a couple, Fred?"

"A couple. Two."

"Really? Two weeks ago you talked to her?"

"Shit. Maybe it's been three. Maybe four."

"How did she sound?"

"Like she was having the time of her life. What if she is doing porn? I've read that the porn industry is huge there, well regulated."

This was the problem, that Fred didn't really see one. Pat wanted to reach down his throat and rip out his heart. "You text me or call me if she contacts you. Promise me that you will." Why was she bothering? His promises meant next to nothing.

"Sure," he said. "I've got to get back to work." He and Marc managed a team of mostly large, sedentary men who hauled tons of stuff great distances in enormous rigs. He was still svelte in his mid-forties. She was, too, but to different effect. She hated that men, in the aggregate, aged better than women. Especially gay men. When they were twenty-one, he'd swept her off her feet with his good looks and manners and dress. His hair had always been perfect. He'd never mauled her; she, more often than he, had initiated sex, and it had always been delightfully slow and in absolute darkness. Fred had required absolute darkness.

The father of a former client, Bob had been her lover for three years. They lived comfortably apart, came together less and less frequently but were a comfort to one another even, or especially, when they were apart. She could depend on Bob.

"It could be bullshit," Bob opined for the fifth time since they'd headed to the Louis Armstrong International Airport. Bob owned Bob's Cajun Kitchen in Old Metairie. From old money, he didn't really need to work but loved to cook.

"Then why hasn't she called? Why hasn't she emailed?"

"I'm just saying, it could be bullshit."

Bob's daughter had been a cutter. She'd stopped cutting a few months into therapy, but Pat figured the girl had simply grown out of that particular destructive behavior. Bob and Pat had tried to get their girls together a couple of times but to more or less disastrous effect. Melanie, despite the pizzazz of her former affliction, had been a wan, translucent adolescent; Missy always possessed star quality. A beautiful girl, Missy turned heads and entertained everyone in her sphere. She'd been a fag hag since she was Shirley Temple, which is what Fred's gay brigade had tagged her when she was eight.

As she retrieved her bag from the trunk of Bob's Lexus, as she shouldered her carry-on and kissed Bob perfunctorily, the image of Missy second-lining with Fred and Marc and several dark men at Mardi Gras four years ago emerged from the chaos of her thoughts. It was a crystalline image; the photo that captured that moment was on her nightstand. Her mixed-race daughter dancing with her white daddy and his whiter partner, the three of them pumping umbrellas, high-stepping on St. Louis Street in the Quarter, always made Pat happy, hopeful, even, though she couldn't exactly say why.

She and Fred had travelled abroad with three-year-old Missy in the mid-nineties; in Paris they'd felt comfortable, in Vienna only a little less so. In Prague, they'd attracted unabashed stares. Pat had known the unease of being othered; it happened almost everywhere, even in New Orleans. But the othering she'd experienced among the Czech Slavs had felt of an entirely different order.

The world was changing. Missy, a gorgeous young woman of color, could look up to a national leader whose skin and hair were like hers. Even when she was othered she did not feel that way, did not accept it. She'd dated both black and white males, did not prefer one to the other, actually said once that she didn't notice much difference. Both light boys and dark boys (her father had insisted when she was very young that she couch the difference thusly) wanted sex more than anything. Both would do just about anything to have sex with a beautiful female.

"It's all chemistry," Missy once said, laughing. "Guys just want to be all in my smooth little cha-cha!"

"Smooth?" Pat had said, perplexed.

"Mama, you don't shave your coochie? I don't know any girls who don't shave down there!"

Well, shaving her pussy had never even occurred to Pat. Clearly, it was a generational thing.

Missy's promiscuity had been, generationally speaking, hardly excessive. She'd had sex with a dozen or so guys, and favored men ten to twenty years her senior for the obvious reason that by that time of life males had finally learned how to pleasure women, but weren't too old yet to "perform." She was very practical about the whole matter. She'd remain loyal to a guy until he started assuming ownership, and at that point cut him loose. Pat actually admired her daughter's attitude toward sex and her attitude toward male authority. When Missy had decided to attend Anglo-American University in Prague, it had been in the wake of her breaking a very sensitive, thirty-year-old white kid's heart. A lawyer who'd finally passed the Louisiana bar on the third try, he'd been a public defender working for little more than candy bars and toilet paper. He'd been poorer than a college student, but loved Missy fiercely, and she'd found him amusing, but not so amusing that she'd put up with his increasing clinginess. She'd cut him loose one stormy summer evening in Chalmette where he inexplicably lived in the midst of seven-year-old Katrina ruin, and he'd shot himself in the mouth the following weekend at his parents' house across the river in Algiers. Missy had just needed to "get the fuck out of New Orleans" for a while, and, after enrolling online for her sophomore year at AAU, with the plan of transferring those credits back to Tulane, she'd jetted off to middle Europe with absolutely no concern for how she would be regarded there as a tall, svelte, gorgeous young woman of color who owned her mother's hair.

Can you give me any more details? Pat had emailed Missy's roommate, but had received no reply.

Pat knew her daughter's address. She'd contacted the school, but AAU would not give out information on the phone or by email. Missy was a legal adult, and as it turned out had not listed Pat as someone to contact in an emergency. Was there an emergency? Was Missy missing? She asked the secretary, the gatekeeper, on the phone, if Missy were attending classes and was informed in no uncertain terms that that was information the secretary was not obliged to give out without the student's permission.

Raised by her single mother and grandmother in the lower Ninth Ward, Pat despaired at ever being able to recover her ancestral home from the devastation of the great storm of 2005. It remained intact if utterly ruined, and the neighborhood, the cluster of ancestral homes, of black families that reached back three, four, five generations, would never be reestablished. Now, she owned, uptown on Zimple, a shotgun that Fred had bought outright and signed over to her in the divorce. It was in a part of town that would never flood, or, if it ever did, the entire city would be devastated beyond Katrina, beyond Pat's own considerable imagination.

Wet Spot, Missy's addled Chihuahua/toy-poodle mix—Fred had named it upon handing the puppy over to her when she was seven—had run away from the Days Inn in Shreveport where Pat and twelve-year-old Missy, who'd just finished her first period, had waited out Katrina. Fred had pulled strings to secure them the room the day before Katrina made landfall. They'd caravanned at roughly the speed of ancient caravans, bumper to desperate bumper, and made it to the motel on empty. Wet Spot stealthily broke away from the room, negotiated stairs, and galloped, Pat had assumed, into the adjacent weedy field. Missy had wept into the night after hours of wading through weeds calling the little rat's name. Pat had thought it best to leave her daughter alone, so took an Ambien at seven and vacated the room and the world. When she'd awakened at four in the morning, Missy had been spooning Rocky Road from a quart container, watching porn on the television; a slim fellow covered in nondescript tattoos had been hammering his enormous member into a pasty blonde's anus. The exuberant couple had seemed to be occupying a room very similar to the Days Inn Pat and Missy occupied.

"My God, child, what are you watching?" Missy had perched at the end of the bed.

"What does it look like I'm watching?"

"Turn that trash off!"

"I'd never take it up the ass," had been Missy's nonchalant reply. "Found Wet Spot!" she'd continued, muting the porn and licking the spoon.

Hands behind, supporting her torso in an upright position in the bed, Pat had surveyed the room. By the door had lain a bundle of blood-soaked towels. Something had mauled the little creature in the weeds, devoured part of him.

Of course Pat could not sleep on the transatlantic flight. She sat next to a little towhead, perhaps five years old, who was separated from his mother seated two rows ahead. An ancient sari-garbed asshole from the subcontinent had mysteriously refused to switch seats with the child, and Pat felt an uneasy duty to attend to the boy, once even walking him to the bathroom and watching from the cracked door as he negotiated his little wiener from his shorts and put it back again. Pat had wanted a son, which is not to say that she hadn't wanted a daughter; she simply wished that Missy had grown up with a brother. The years after her divorce she'd sought strong black men for relationships, but nothing had clicked. With one, she'd considered getting impregnated quite independent of his volition. He'd been a Loyola history professor, married with kids, and Pat had considered the situation perfect for a sperm donation but, alas, the professor had been preternaturally careful, and could not be persuaded to have sex without a condom.

"Are you from Africa?" the little blonde asked. Such a question suggested precociousness. How should she answer?

"What do you think Africa is?"

The child stared at the back of the seat in front of him. "Daddy says Africa is where black people come from."

"Well, I'm from America, like you. My people came to America from Africa a long time ago. Do you know where your people came from?"

The child was perplexed. "We come from Chicago," he said, finally.

"Well, yes, but your people came from somewhere else. They probably came from Europe."

"What's that?"

"It's where we're going. It's where this plane is taking us."

"We're going to Oslo."

"And Oslo is in Europe, like Chicago is in Illinois, and Illinois is in America."

He was puzzled. "We're going to Oslo to get my new sister."

One traveled to China, Russia, Romania to extract children from hellish childcare facilities, but Norway? There was a complex story here, one Pat didn't wish to coax out. She smiled and feigned sleep.

Through passport control, she found her bag almost immediately and pushed into the bustling terminal. She spotted an ATM, a "Bankomat," and used her Visa to acquire five thousand koruna, about two hundred and fifty dollars. The cab ride wasn't particularly informative as to how much the place had changed since her visit in the mid-nineties. Pat simply couldn't recall much of the trip beyond the bridge, the castle, the river, spires, Old Town Square and its famous clock, a uniquely hilly topography. Within the haze of time, she recalled that the city was comparatively inexpensive, and that Czechs had stared at her and her child on trams and on the Metro. They'd stared in restaurants and on the tourist-clotted streets. One way she'd been able to delineate tourists from Czechs was that the former, for the most part, hadn't stared.

It was eleven in the morning local time, five in the morning as far as her body was concerned. She had a vague idea that the hotel was located behind the castle, but when the cab pulled up to it she was put off by the architecture. Yes, it was kind of pyramid-like, but it was a hideous design. She'd read about communist-era architecture, the vain attempts to create hip, super-modern structures whose final effects were simply goofy.

The lobby of the goofy building was less hideous, even a little charming. There were whimsical touches, such as cast-iron statues in the bar/lounge that resembled Picasso's drawings of Don Quixote. The plastic foliage everywhere was kind of cute.

Pat slept like death and awoke with a start. It took several seconds to realize where she was. It was 7 p.m. by the room clock. She would not get back to sleep. She rose, showered, and dressed.

She showed Missy's address to a severely pretty woman at the desk. The bleach-blonde instructed Pat to take the 22 tram to Malostranská, then to transfer to the 17.

For the brief time that Fred, Missy, and Pat had been a family, their bond in public had been purely defensive. They were a mixed-race couple raising a mixed-race child and all the world seemed a stage to that fact. The audience gawked beyond the almost blinding footlights. "Because they were physically striking—the white, handsome, immaculately groomed father; the statuesque, Nefertiti-beautiful mother; and the otherworldly pretty, exotic child—the gawking had been that much more intense. And of course on those occasions of insult or outright threat, Fred had wilted, offered no psychic or physical protection. On trips to San Diego to visit Fred's extended family, in Texas diners where big men wearing big hats commented frankly and loudly about race, Fred had never offered any defense. Had it been fair for Pat to want Fred to defend her and their child from verbal abuse?

"Hey, cocksucker!" Pat had once exploded. "We can fucking hear you, you racist piece of shit! Why don't you and I go outside, motherfucker!" Fred had tugged at her blouse. The three men had cracked up at the situation, the gender role reversal.

The family had moved on to another diner a hundred miles down Interstate 10, to more hateful stares, more unabashed, derogatory commentary.

The early evening was quite bright. Pat's back ached from the long flight, and her ankles were swollen; every little lurch of the tram shot pain through her lower back. As the 22 snaked down toward the river, three German boys surfed backwards in the aisle, holding straps for balance and staring at Pat; they spoke in normal voices, smiled what seemed to Pat wicked smiles. "Are you a movie star?" the taller of the three said in slow, perfect English.

"Would I be riding a fucking streetcar if I were a movie star?" Pat shot back. Her interlocutor looked wounded. Perhaps he was just trying to be nice. Perhaps he was indeed mistaking Pat for someone he'd seen in a movie. "No, I'm not a movie star," she said slowly, "and please don't stare at me. It makes me uncomfortable."

The boys' smiles had not been wicked, after all. Their smiles now faded into head-bowed, chastened expressions. They remained on the tram when Pat got off at Malostranská.

Before going to Missy's apartment, or what Pat hoped was still her apartment, Pat would check out her single lead. Missy wrote once that she frequented an expat hangout called the Old Globe. Using the map she'd procured from the hotel desk, Pat hiked down to the Legií Bridge, crossed the Vltava, scooted behind the National Theater, then several blocks to the bookstore/café.

The English-language bookstore was in front, and the café in the rear. Pat felt immediately safe, oddly at home. Folks chattered in English all around. The place was arty, funky, cool. Old-school jazz filled the air, low enough to allow comfortable conversation. She introduced herself to the tall, dumpy, affable American working the bar.

"Oh, yeah, Missy comes here almost every day. She usually sits over there, in the corner, and works on her laptop."

"Do you remember when she was here last?"

Mike stroked his goatee. "Yeah, I'm pretty sure she was in yesterday. She gets here at about nine, like I said, just about every weekday."

It was 8:40. "Do you mean nine a.m. or p.m.?"

"I work four to one on days we close at one, four to midnight otherwise. She usually closes us down."

Pat ordered a vodka tonic, assumed a table in the darkest corner of the room, below the stairs to the upper level. "I'm her mother," she told Mike when he brought her drink.

"Figured," he answered, smiling.

When Missy was nine, a year after the divorce, Pat took her to the Audubon Zoo almost every weekend. The redundancy, the verdant familiarity of that beautiful zoo, one of the jewels of the city, had been comforting to them both. Missy had been shuttling between two homes due to a joint custody arrangement Pat could have kicked herself in the ass for agreeing to, and Pat's nerves had been more or less irreparably frayed; the zoo had been a place of healing.

"Look, Mama, they're fucking!" Missy had exclaimed. A clutch of children and their parents, white, black, and Asian, swiveled their shocked heads toward her. She'd pointed not into a primate habitat, but at a tree, a young oak, where, indeed, two gray squirrels had been going at it no more than thirty feet away on a low branch. The male would get started and the female would break away and scoot forward; the male would again mount her only to suffer the female's demure three-step scuttling forward. Again he'd mount her.

Pat had laughed against her will; she'd touched her breast, thrown back her head, and guffawed. She'd laughed so hard her eyes had filled with tears, and when she'd blinked away her mirth, the squirrels had still been at it *doggie style*, and she laughed harder; finally, she'd taken Missy's hand and led her away from primates, toward reptiles.

It seemed counterintuitive, but the long walk had actually served to bring the swelling down in her ankles. She sipped her drink, pretended to study the artwork on the walls, images that seemed too cute, too clever, too cool. Pat knew that she should not be there. When she'd last spoken with Missy on the phone they'd argued about money, about Fred not holding up his end, as usual. Missy was simply pissed at her; that's why she hadn't called, hadn't answered emails.

When they'd finally been allowed to return to New Orleans, when they'd finally worked up the nerve to enter the lower Ninth Ward to survey the damage to their ancestral home, they'd driven down St. Claude and turned onto Charbonnet, crossed Claiborne to Derbigny. The streets had been littered with all manner of debris, mostly tree limbs. Their renters had phoned, declared the two-story, eighty-year-old structure uninhabitable. Indeed, the entire neighborhood had been, as Pat and Missy had witnessed in shocked silence on their slow drive, utterly uninhabitable. Pat had wept silently down Derbigny onto Roman. Missy had stroked her mother's arm as they'd entered the house in which Pat had grown up, in which her mother and her mother's mother had been born, and the knowledge of the end of something good and beautiful had soaked into Pat and Missy's hearts.

Missy stood stock-still before her mother's table. She'd let her hair grow out a bit, and she had a white streak dyed down the middle. She wore a green Tulane T-shirt that was a size too small. She was braless, and her breasts declared themselves through the green fabric.

"I hear that the Prague Zoo is worth a visit," Pat said. Missy was frozen. "No judgment," Pat said. "No judgment, I promise. Just go to the zoo with me, baby."

Missy relaxed, slowly, thawed. She stared at her mother and smelled her grandmother's red beans cooking on a Monday afternoon when she was five, then the mold in the wood of her dead grandmother's house when Missy was twelve. She stared into her mother's eyes and saw her grandmother holding Pat's weeping head against her breast, and she saw her own naked, womanly body dancing ecstatically and alone.

Rye Bread

2010

Mack was not particularly fond of his Czech in-laws. They were as boring as his own American family, whom he did not so much dislike as found easy to dismiss. He'd met Marie, "Mařenka," as her family called her, in graduate school at Tulane. She'd been a graduate exchange student of postmodern southern American literature; he'd been ABD, finishing his dissertation on southern decorum and its influence on second-and third-generation southern confessional poets.

Marie's mother was a buxom, quite fetching municipal judge in her early fifties. Her father was a failed novelist living primarily off the proceeds from restituted property he'd sold much too cheaply in the '90s. He was remarried to an office mouse who worshipped him and mumbled when she spoke Czech or broken English. Judge Mama, as Mack called Hana Nováková to his wife, was coupled with an innocuous retired civil engineer twenty years her senior. Mack thought Josef was a hoot. His wavy, naturally black hair was always perfectly combed, and he knocked back a shot of Slivovice every morning at breakfast, and drank beer, slowly and steadily, from eleven in the morning until ten at night when he went to bed. He spoke no English, but smiled at Mack a lot, and was a terrific cook.

Mack and Marie had spent June, July, and half of August in Prague each of the seven years of their marriage. Both were "retained" instructors teaching three freshman composition courses and one sophomore literature course every semester at New Orleans State University. They were desperately looking for tenure-track gigs elsewhere, though neither wanted to leave the Big Easy, the good life there. A "retained instructor" was stuck in rank below assistant professor possibly for an entire career, no matter how much and/or how well she or he published. Between them, they earned enough to live comfortably in the upper Ninth Ward and to spend summers in Prague, but apparently not enough to have a child, an absence Judge Mama referred to often and unsubtly.

Josef and his cronies smoked and drank beer at a long picnic table under an enormous ginkgo. They were shirtless and old-man gross, but they owned their sagging bellies and chinless faces such that they were beautiful. A small pig roasted in an oilcan jerry-rigged contraption. The oldest of the crew of seven rose every few minutes to baste and turn the impaled carcass. Mack sat in a lawn chair shirtless, soaking up rays, re-reading the introduction to *The Poetics of Space*; the muted strains of masculine Czech chatter and laughter were like polka music through an ancient transistor radio. Josef's *chata*, country cottage, was nestled among dozens of others on a lush, gentle hill forty minutes from Prague. Mack could never figure out how almost every Czech he knew afforded such a bucolic retreat, though life in the Czech lands, he'd come to realize, in spring and summer had always rotated on a city/country axis.

Marie and Judge Mama were arguing in the cabin, never raising their voices but seeming more antagonistic for their control. Judge Mama wanted a grandchild, and she wanted Marie and Mack to move to Prague permanently.

The prospect of moving to Prague permanently was distasteful to Mack, even though he and Marie had learned before the weekend that the Faculty of Arts of Charles University would hire them to teach in its study abroad program. The money wouldn't be as good even as what they earned as bottom-feeding instructors at a third-rate institution such as NOSU, but their housing would be free; Judge Mama had been restituted a forty-unit, seven-story apartment building in the early '90s, and had given Marie and Mack a nice two-bedroom on the ground floor as a wedding gift. They would sometimes sublet it for the months they were working in New Orleans, but this past year did not.

Mack had published four refereed articles, one in *PMLA*, from chapters of his dissertation. He'd been finishing the monograph he'd adapted from his dissertation for six years, eliciting praise from more than half of the anonymous referees, contempt or tepid dismissal from the rest. By the early 2000s, no one really wanted to read anything about confessional poetry, even or especially such ego-drenched stuff composed by southerners. The subject was as passé as a sitcom laugh track, though not nearly as enduring.

After months of doldrums, of acidic self-pity, he was finally rebounding. He was bringing a new article to fruition, one that he was certain would be the heart of a new book manuscript. He'd discovered an early twentieth-century Louisiana poet whose work had never been published and whom Mack was certain was one of the finest lyric poets of the century. That Archibald McKinsey had been black, had been childhood friends with Buddy Bolden, and had been shot dead in a whorehouse at the Christ-y age of thirty-three only enhanced his value.

Mack had been goofing through the stacks of the used bookstore on Dauphine in the Quarter when he'd fetched a purple spine from a high shelf, and had been startled that the pages had not been covered with print, but with small, elegant, starkly legible handwriting, some in fountain pen, some in pencil. Mack had of course produced a typed script of the poems very early on, fearful that the penciled texts in particular would smudge into illegibility as the result of his frequent perusals.

Mac remembered sitting in the Café du Monde, reading the book from cover to cover, and feeling, as Emily Dickinson had said one should, as though the top of his head were blown off. After much frantic digging, good old-fashion scholarly nitpicking, he'd pieced together Archibald McKinsey's story, at least in broad outline. An autodidact, McKinsey had worked in an über rich uptown home as a butler of sorts from 1892 to 1904, following his own father in that position. He'd had access to a rich merchant's glorious library his entire life; Maurice Topper, heir to one of the most profitable shipping companies in North America, had witnessed "Archie's" inquisitiveness and prodigious verbal facility from when the lad was first toddling along the balcony of what a generation earlier had been the "slave quarters." Topper had eventually opened his library to the child, the boy, the man, and McKinsey had devoured the classics, and then the great English and American novels and many anthologies of English-language verse.

"You . . . want . . . some . . . Miss . . . Piggy?" Josef asked Mack, forming each word lugubriously yet sporting an enormous grin. His six buddies guffawed, Mack assumed more at the fact that their friend had managed a sentence in English than at the delightfully odd reference to the Muppet icon.

"Pozdě," Mack answered, smiling back. He would wait for Marie; they would fill paper plates with succulent flesh, tomato wedges, day-old rye bread, and stroll out to the adjacent meadow to eat and chat.

Mack had pondered the phrase "wry bread" in one of McKinsey's Petrarchan sonnets; at first Mack had assumed that the poet had simply misspelled *rye,* but had come to understand that it was not a misspelling at all. The poet was anthropomorphizing bread, "the staff of life," as did Jesus Christ when on several occasions in the Bible He likened Himself to bread. McKinsey, Mack believed, throughout his work encoded a reading of scripture that rendered Christ as a kind of Jewish comedian, Groucho Marx, with healing powers and a master plan.

Judge Mama stormed out of the cabin and strode determinedly toward Mack. Marie followed frowning, castigating her mother in rapid-fire Czech. Judge Mama stood before Mack, hands on hips. She was much prettier than her daughter, but was also a shrill, single-minded dynamo who inserted herself into matters that were none of her fucking business.

"Why you don't want child?" she asked, seemingly on the verge of tears.

"It's none of your fucking business, Hana," he answered with no malice in his voice, only weariness.

"Why do you marry if you do not want baby?"

Mack gazed over her shoulder at Marie, slowly shook his head. "You ready to eat?" he asked Marie.

"Yeah, babe," she responded, smiling sadly.

Hana then spoke to him as if he could understand her, though she knew he could not. The fact that they couldn't understand each other beyond the most basic discourse had been a happy circumstance for Mack.

"Tell her there are too many people in the world," he said. "Tell her I'm a selfish man-cunt who wants you all to myself. Tell her we both love our work, that our students are our children. Tell her I don't want to watch you get fat. Tell her I just don't like kids."

"She knows all that," Marie said, as weary of her mother's intrusions as was Mack. He rose from the chair, dog-eared the page he was reading, and placed the paperback where he'd sat. He took two slow steps and embraced his mother-in-law. She hugged him back. He did not dislike her or like her; he was simply tired of her harping. He felt an odd compassion for her, for the intensity with which she seemed to feel the burden of her mortality. A baby would fill the void between "rye" and "wry," between the world and the word, between judgment and cosmic acquiescence.

But of course it would not.

He licked his fingers, chewed some crispy skin. The bread was not too stale to eat, but he did not want it. The pig and tomatoes were enough. He tossed pinches of the creamy-gray Czech bread toward a tuft of dandelion; two, then three then four intrepid sparrows feasted. A McKinsey couplet hovered above the ringing in his ears:

The Child of Wonder is not wonderful.
He gnaws each grimace of the pitiful.

It didn't represent the best of McKinsey, and yet it resonated in that moment. "Marie, why don't you just tell her?"

Marie remained fixed on the sparrows.

"I'm not ashamed," Mack said.

"I know. I'm not either, babe. I just don't think she could handle it."

Born Macy Adams, Mack had been post-op for twelve years. He had lived through two puberties, as Macy, then as Mack. His father, oddly, had been the supportive parent; his mother had been, and remained, mortified. His older sister, a midlife born-again, looked upon him as though he were a steaming pile of dog shit. She'd literally scowled the entire time he was ever in her presence.

Marie and Mack had married in New Orleans by virtue of the fact that Mack had been able to change his gender and name on his birth certificate. The law, recently clarified, had been murky seven years ago, but, as is true regarding so many things in New Orleans, the proper alignment of personalities in positions of authority may accomplish just about anything. To change name and gender on a Louisiana birth certificate, one must submit a legal petition that includes a surgeon's letter that "diagnoses the individual as a transsexual or pseudo-hermaphrodite, and details that sex reassignment or corrective surgery has been properly performed upon the petitioner." Well, it certainly helped that his doctor's brother was a (closeted) gay judge. What had taken others excruciating months of exorbitant legal fees clicked into place in mere days and at practically no cost. Mack would be paying off the $70,000-plus price of the operation for many years, but the monthly payment was manageable, and his hormone regime was covered by the excellent health plan of his university.

Of one hundred and forty-seven poems in Archibald McKinsey's hand-written book, two thirds were sonnets and the rest in either blank or free verse. The free verse poems strongly suggest the influence of Whitman, though *Leaves of Grass* had not at that time been widely accessible. Some of the free verse even suggested a familiarity with William Carlos Williams, though Mack knew that that was impossible given the dates. Perhaps Archibald had simply caught wind of imagism and somehow channeled the spirit of the good doctor. Getting access to the Topper library would be a priority upon their return to New Orleans.

Marie traced with her right index finger the red dragon that spanned his muscular chest and hid the mastectomy scars. She'd accompanied him when he'd gotten it near the beginning of their relationship. It was an intricate, fiercely sexy dragon, deep red with bright yellow eyes and golden highlights. It had taken four three-hour sessions.

He threw the last of his bread to the squad of sparrows. Marie rubbed the stubble on his chin, smiled. "Let's tell her tonight," she said.

Mack was taken aback. "Well, basically, all I can do is sit there and grin. You'll have to do all the telling. She'll be shocked, and then, after we administer smelling salts, she'll have a thousand questions. I don't think we should tell Josef. That should be her call."

Laughter erupted from the clutch of old men; one was mocking another to the utter delight of all. It was Josef's seventy-fourth birthday, and each June 23rd he roasted a pig at his *chata*. This was Mack's sixth pig day at Josef's country cabin.

"Yeah, I'll think about it a little more."

"Hey, it's your call. She's your Judge Mama. You're the one who'll have to deal with her wigging out."

They'd arrived at the *chata* with Hana in her Škoda, but had decided even before they'd arrived that they'd return by train. The station was a forty-minute walk, and it felt good to move after the heavy, meaty meal.

Marie was segueing out of southern lit and was trying to earn some cred as a composition specialist, though she had no formal training in the field. She figured, though, that if she scored some decent publications in the field, or at least on the fringe of it, she and Mack would be more marketable as a couple. They discussed her present project, a study of course-ending "proficiency exams" within composition pedagogy, particularly regarding "modes of discourse." Mack didn't just hate, he fucking hated his department's proficiency exam, one in which, at the end of a semester, individuals other than the classroom instructor determined if a student passed the course. Mack judged the entire contraption as flying in the face of the very idea of academic freedom, but as a bottom-feeding retained instructor did not dare rock that particular bureaucratic boat. He believed in speaking truth to power, and had indeed done so on numerous occasions in his life, but was wise enough not to fall on career-killing swords. That little bureaucracy that so vexed him he'd decided years ago to regard as benign.

Archibald McKinsey dedicated two quite ironic Elizabethan sonnets to his childhood buddy Buddy Bolden. The boys had palled around when they were ten, eleven, and twelve, according to the diary of Topper's wife, Betsy Topper née Fitzgerald. Someone in the family had transferred the daily journal to microfiche and it somehow ended up in the Loyola library. Betsy Topper had been as fond of Archie as her husband had been, and both had been quite progressive for their day. She had referred daily to the "little scamp" spending hours in the library, "quiet as a ghost," and there are numerous references to his only friend, a wild child named Buddy Bolden. How the boys had met, what they'd done together and how often and when were details that had not risen to her notice, and that Archie's Buddy may not have been *the* Buddy of course had crossed Mack's mind, but he would move heaven, earth, and entire archives for evidence that the world-class poet he'd singularly discovered had indeed been the boyhood chum of the father of jazz.

There are no recordings of Buddy Bolden, only the recorded interviews of men and women who'd heard him play his cornet. Mack had read Ondaatje's *Coming Through Slaughter* years ago, found it charming, quite beautifully written, but not much help. It is, after all, a novel about a great musician whose greatness is pure legend. The strains of Satchmo's horn, his incredible voice, will live on into the explosion of the sun; Bolden's madness is a matter of record. His genius, and its dynamic relation to his madness, is a matter of pure conjecture. His effect on everything that came after, including Armstrong, is one of the mysteries of modern art.

But Mack possessed the poems, in the poet's own hand, of an artist of equal genius, genius the value of which was not its effect but the very fact of its existence.

Marie napped with her head on his shoulder. At a backwater stop, twenty minutes from Prague, five plastered skinheads piled into their compartment. Marie awoke with a start. They passed a bottle of the cheapest vodka. Their eyes were bloodshot, their boyish faces flushed. They were fraternal joy and threat. They were not large, but they were hard. Mack's shirt was buttoned to just below his solar plexus; a kid wearing a faded Alice in Chains T-shirt, probably handed down to him by an older brother, peered down Mack's shirt, seeming to try to get a better look at the dragon. He said something and the pod laughed.

"What'd he say?" Mack half whispered. But before Marie could answer, another kid, shirtless, shoeless, more drunk than the others, slurred something that invoked more mirth, then he climbed up on the opposite seat, pushed down the window, pulled out his penis and pissed. Some of it splashed back into the compartment by the wind of the train's movement, landing in Marie's face as a light spray.

Mack shot up, grabbed the kid who still held his penis, and threw him onto the floor of the compartment. The kid's shaved head bounced on the hard surface.

"Nigger lover," one of them not so much shouted as simply and firmly asserted.

The kid on the floor rose gingerly to his ass, held his knees with one hand, the back of his head with the other. The conductor slid open the door to the compartment and dressed down the boys. They exited one by one as the train came to its penultimate stop. When they were out of sight the conductor checked Mack's and Marie's tickets, and Marie followed him to clean her face in the funky toilet room between cars.

The mid-teen kid who'd hurled the epithet had recognized American English, and had reasoned that a white American who takes umbrage at someone pissing out a train window will of course be simpatico with black Americans. Skinheads' jumbled neo-Nazi ideology focused hatred on Roma, but they also hated, or thought they did, Jews, Moslems, and all people of color, including Asians. That kid had probably never seen an African American in the flesh in his life. He'd only seen them in movies, on American TV shows that got dubbed into Czech.

Decades before *Invisible Man*, Archibald McKinsey wrote,

You tether my shadow to a drop of rain
And whip that empty darkness 'til it screams.
You hate me perfectly when I'm not there.
Your hatred renders me invisible,
Like any ordinary Holy Ghost.

"You okay, doll?"

"Hey, what girl doesn't like a golden shower now and again?"

When the train pulled in, it was pushing nine but still quite bright out. They took the C-line to Pražského povstání and strolled the quarter mile toward home.

"Do you think he's a great poet?" Mack asked.

"I don't think he's as great as you think he is, but I think he was remarkable for his time and circumstances," Marie answered. "But hey, you're the poetry scholar, and my judgment of English-language verse is always a little skewed because I'm not a native speaker. There's something visceral about poetry, even the poetry of literary prose, that clamps it to the guts of native speakers."

"Conrad, Nabokov," he countered.

"Yeah, okay. Conrad and Nabokov were Conrad and Nabokov"— she smiled. "But listen, even if others don't think he's a major talent, he's still one hell of a find, certainly worth articles, certainly worth a book." After a brief, easy silence, she asked for the first time in their years together, "Why don't you write poetry, Mack?"

He was startled by the question. She knew quite well his contempt for most people who call themselves poets.

Their favorite Vietnamese vendor was tending to the tomatoes, cucumbers, peppers, melons, grapes, apples, seedy little tangerines piled in bins along the busy window of his tiny, packed store. He beamed at them as they entered, and followed them in. They purchased a bottle of the clear fruit liquor that Mack favored, and a bottle of the Moravian red, Frankovka, that Marie drank. They ambled the remaining two blocks to Judge Mama's building, their Prague home.

"Why don't you write poetry?" she asked again.

"I did."

"My God, when?"

"Before I began the change. Before I met you."

"Did you keep them?"

"I burned them in a huge aluminum trash can when I burned all of the stuff of her life, her clothes, her undergarments, her books, her photos, especially those, I also burned her poems. They were mere juvenilia. She had no idea what she was expressing. She had no idea that her poems all screamed that she wanted to be me."

"You should think of her as your daughter," Marie said. "You should love her and nurture her."

"She's dead."

"No, she isn't, babe. Archibald McKinsey is dead. There are dead poets and living ones. We have to learn to love the living poets, even the ones whose poems are terrible or young or both. You should write poems to your daughter, babe."

"Is she our daughter?"

"Yes."

Mack would come to realize that Archibald McKinsey was not a great poet, only an interesting one and for reasons that had nothing to do with whether Archie's boyhood companion had been the great and tragic musician; McKinsey was interesting because he'd been black and brilliant and educated himself at a time and in a place wholly incompatible with that heroic achievement. Mack would come to realize that all poetry is spiritual subterfuge that at its best and its worst touches the divine. He would come to realize that the red dragon on his chest was the mother of his pride.

As his beloved entered their apartment ahead of him, something inside of him was missing, that sliver of bitterness he'd always thought to be the cutting edge of his masculinity. That bitterness would return again and again, but for now it was gone and he did not miss it. He felt no less a man without his bitterness, just a tiny bit sadder.

"I'll be right in, doll," he told his wife as she entered their bedroom.

He pressed his left hand against the wall behind the receptacle, lifted the seat, assumed the position, and pissed luxuriously.

The Hunger Wall

1997

It is not so revered as the Wailing Wall, or as forbidding as the Berlin Wall once was, though it is as physically innocuous as the former and as buffeted by the stinking winds of political vagaries as the latter. People were starving. Charlie 4 paid them to build a useless wall, the story goes. It was a public works project. The Great Wall is visible from space, the Hunger Wall from certain angles even only a mile away. It keeps in nothing, keeps out nothing.

In a clearing beyond the first rise, where the cement walkway doubles back along the angle of the Hunger Wall, Luella glanced through shadow-dappled leaves a skinny gypsy boy masturbating vigorously. His expression was that of a fervently praying saint. She stared a moment, then continued her descent.

She'd fallen in love with Jan back in San Diego and followed him to Prague. The ten weeks she'd occupied the city were the core of spring, and she was enthralled by Prague's transformation out of purgatorial drabness. The image of the concupiscent boy—shorts around his knees, dingy too-big T-shirt held up by his free hand—was consistent with the lushness of the broad Petřín Hill which, taken with the Vltava along whose east bank it lay, set back less than half a kilometer, dominated the topography of the city.

Czechs stared at her; she was used to being stared at, but not dispassionately. In America, black men stared at her with unambiguous lust, and most white men with furtive, awful lust. The Czechs, men and women, seemed to stare as one might at a fanning peacock come suddenly into view, with a muted, startled delight free, at first, of desire. Six-feet-two, slimly voluptuous, with a face whose features blended her father's African oval beauty with her Asian mother's exquisiteness, Luella Silverlake Jones did not doubt that she was the most exotic living thing in Prague that season.

And indeed she was a thing, a moving object the vortex of whose image drew regard into every visual frame she entered. A professional model since the age of fifteen, she'd lived better than most of her fellow students at the University of California at Santa Barbara, and even as she'd grown used to being a professional image, she'd looked forward to the day she could be something else, a doctor of something or other, an authority on something and not just an exotic, un-ignorable presence defining any landscape it happens to occupy.

A Czech movie director visiting his Czech-American fashion-photographer cousin, Jan had been the first man ever to ignore her. Even gay men fixated longingly upon her, though always such as to render her a projected subject rather than an object of desire. Jan, a plain, sandy-haired, sallow, middle-aged man with a thick accent she could not identify, had appeared at a Venice Beach shoot with a representative of the agency, and had exhibited animated enthusiasm for the sand and water, color and noise, and absolutely no interest in her own dark, bikinied form. While the photographer, and even the other models fawned over her between camera clicks, and everyone on the beach swiped glances as they lounged and crisped in the California sun, Jan chattered barely comprehensibly about the waves, the likes of which he'd only seen in movies, and about the thick dance of almost naked forms lying, skating, surfing, patting white balls over gossamer nets, or simply drooping against one another along the low wall between the sand and cement.

She'd been drawn to his voice, a concoction of cream and chartreuse over crushed ice, a startling incongruity that charmed. She'd introduced herself to him at a break, and he'd smiled and pumped her hand. "You are very beautiful," he'd said, and though a thousand men and almost as many women had said the same words to her ten thousand times, she'd never heard it said so distractedly. The photographer's cousin, he'd begun his first visit to America less than an hour earlier when he'd been gathered, rumpled and weary, from LAX and swept to the shoot. Luella had offered to show him around, and over that weekend had seen everything through his eyes, especially herself. She'd liked how he regarded the city, other Americans, and her. She'd liked how he'd spoken English, the raspy, high-pitched, always-on-the-verge-of-laughter way he'd spoken it.

She'd committed to living in Prague through mid-August, and though over two months remained, already she was regretting having to leave. But she had little choice, for there seemed small chance of steady work in Central Europe. Besides, she was also committed to finishing graduate school. Jan had promised that when they returned in August he would remain with her in America if he could find work without their having to resort to a green card marriage. Both of them knew, however, their mutual aversion to the institution of marriage notwithstanding, that with or without a green card he would never find appropriate, or sufficient, employment in America.

Though he was a quite successful filmmaker in Bohemia, Luella knew he wasn't likely to become the next Miloš Forman. She knew that Jan knew he wouldn't be the next Miloš Forman. He would therefore not likely remain with her past November or December, and so a mild melancholy tinged the sweetness of their lives together that spring.

At the end of her descent, on Újezd, Luella caught a 12 tram to Malostranská, and legged the three blocks to the bistro where Jan's younger sister, Nikole, a fairly renowned novelist, was sipping tea, waiting for her.

"Ahoj," Nikole greeted her.

"What does *smrt cikanům*, mean?" Luella said with an odd urgency as she sat down across from the small, bleached-blond, thirtyish author of "women's novels."

"Where did you hear this?" Nikole furrowed her brow.

"I saw a kid write it above the window of a tram. *Smrt* means death, right? The kid looked me in the eye and grinned real nasty after he scrawled it." Luella saw incomprehension in Nicole's expression. "Scrawled . . . wrote it real fast and sloppily. Death what?"

"It means death to gypsies," Nicole said in a hoarse whisper.

As is true of most Americans, Luella knew little about gypsies beyond the broadest cultural myths, those which portray the *Romové* as swarthy, peripatetic lovers of life, adorable thieves banging tambourines and casting sexy shadows around campfires as they dance under eternally full moons. On her first trip to Europe several years earlier, before the atrocities in the Balkans, she'd spent part of a week in Belgrade. It had seemed the least impressive of major European capitals she'd thus far visited, and she'd been told that before the refurbishing prompted by Yugoslavia hosting the Conference of Nonaligned Nations just the year before, Belgrade had been even shabbier.

She'd sat one warm evening with her traveling companion, a gay boyfriend from UCSB, sipping Turkish coffee at an outdoor table in the liveliest, most colorful quarter of the city. She recalled that as the darkness of the evening had spread and deepened, and pale lights clicked on along the promenade of the quarter, dark children, as if from cracks in the cement, had suddenly appeared. Filthy, ratty-haired, eyes quick as gnats, they'd shuffled about as if looking for something, as if any second one would shout that she had found it and all the others would rush, cheering as they ran, to see.

A very little one, perhaps five, materialized in the weak-bulb gloom of twilight, and held a paper blossom out to them. Luella's friend had taken the gaudy flower and given the child a hundred dinar note, which, even at that time, only the dawn of hyperinflation, was not much, and the girl's accusing glare had said that she'd known that it wasn't much. Luella had then held out three crinkled greenbacks she'd excavated from the dregs of her purse, and the baby's eyes had lit up as from within.

"A great-great uncle on my father's side was hanged naked by his feet from a willow tree, doused with kerosene, and set on fire," Luella said, looking past her lover's sister to a table of three young guys joking loudly in German over beers and schnitzels. Nikole was startled by Luella's non sequitur. Her silence and troubled eyes seemed to beg for an explanation. "Thousands, tens of thousands of black men in America, right up into this century, had things like that done to them," Luella continued.

"Luella, these things are terrible, but why . . ."

"How many gypsies did the Nazis butcher?" Luella interrupted.

Nikole was annoyed. "Racism is always terrible," she said, "but you should not suggest that the situations in America and here are at all similar. Gypsies choose to be how they are."

"And how is that?" Luella shot back.

"You don't know what they're like." Nikole was flustered.

"They're dirty? They're lazy? They steal? They're uneducated or uneducable? They ruin neighborhoods?"

"Yes, all that you say is true. So I was wrong. You *do* know how they are!" Nikole answered defiantly.

Luella sipped her coffee and smiled. Nikole looked away, a little angry, a little ashamed.

"I saw a gypsy boy, fourteen or fifteen, skinny, very beautiful, really, near the bottom of that old wall by the park."

"Hladová Zeď, it is called the Hunger Wall," Nikole affirmed.

"Why is it called that?"

"There are stupid legends. But it is just a useless wall that goes down a hill. Nothing more."

One of the German boys stared at Luella. It was an ordinary, lustful stare, the kind she'd years ago learned to deflect, control. "How old do you think those boys are?" Luella asked, staring beyond Nikole.

"Should I turn?"

"Sure, look now."

Nikole flicked a glance over her shoulder, then whipped back, flushed. All four had smiled right at her. "Why did you tell me to look?" she yelled in a whisper.

Luella chuckled mischievously. "Twenty-one? Two?"

"Why should you care?"

"Because I wonder about their grandparents," Luella replied, putting on her sunglasses.

"Do you want to know something?" Nikole asked then continued without waiting for an answer, "I have met many Americans since '89, all very different. Old American men and old American women, rich and not so rich. Young ones, too; I met one I am certain is a neo-Nazi, a very rich one from Oklahoma, I think, or Ohio or Omaha. Anyway, I have recently met several American professors who call themselves socialists, then insist upon paying for all the checks with VISA cards. One socialist professor I recall quoting something from *Gourmet Magazine*. She spends her summers in a place called Fort Townsend, in the state of Washington."

"Port Townsend," Luella corrected softly.

"Yes, she owns a second home there. Do you know what that rich socialist has in common with the neo-Nazi from Omaha?"

"I hope you are preparing to tell me," Luella said.

"The world kisses your huge American ass."

Luella broke into laughter.

"You laugh," Nikole continued, "but it is true, and you have no idea what it is like not to be American."

At this assertion Luella ceased laughing.

"Even the French," Nikole continued, "even they kiss Mickey Mouse's charming little American ass as they curse everything he represents, which is precisely what they long for."

"And what is that?" Luella asked, eyeing the largest, boldest German boy who smiled lasciviously, knees spread, facing her.

"Hope. They want it. All of us want it. We want to have sex with your American hope, so we kiss your ass."

"What you're talking about is Euro-American. It isn't me. It isn't non-white America. It certainly isn't black America."

"You stink of it!" Nikole laughed without malice, indeed, with a tone of affection. "You, Luella Silverlake Jones, are drunk with it! I don't believe it is only white. The rhythm of this hope is African. It is jazz and rock'n'roll and gospel. It is often destructive, but it is hope all the same, and it is American, only American." Nikole was glowing with revelation.

"Those boys, that one with the bulge in his American jeans, he wants my hope?" Luella joked, uncomfortable with the high seriousness of the conversation.

"In a manner of speaking," Nikole came back, all seriousness.

"That boy by the Hunger Wall, he was spanking his monkey . . ."

"What does that mean?" Nikole interrupted.

"He was masturbating," Luella explained. "He didn't see me. His eyes were shut tight. Was he imagining things American? Was he fantasizing a big, hopeful burger with fries?"

"Gypsies are beyond hope," Nikole said. "That is their power. It is why they are hated."

Expressionless, Luella stared over Nikole's shoulder through black lenses. Slowly, she extended her right arm in a Nazi salute, then turned her hand palm-up, and slowly made a fist, leaving only her middle finger raised to the sky. "Will he understand this?" she asked in a level voice, smiling.

"The sentiment is universal. And he doesn't deserve that Nazi gesture. He's just a boy with a hard one, that is all."

"Hard on," Luella corrected, still smiling, still pointing her middle finger at the perfect June sky.

Jan would not be back from his shoot in Bratislava until the first of the week, and though Nikole quite enjoyed going out nights with Luella, this particular evening Luella had decided to spend alone. She walked up Peskove to a decrepit rock club called Borat, paid the cover and entered the throat-burning, eye-watering miasma of cigarette gases. Something metallic and nondescript had throbbed from the walls as she'd approached the narrow, three-story building; now, the smoke-thickened air seemed brittle from the absence of such noise, and she heard below the mild and fuzzy ringing of cheap amps many casual voices speaking four distinct languages. A tall boy whose hair was shorn to stubble and whose thin arms were awash in blue-black images of death, passion, and generic disaster, inflicted high school French on a fleecy blond girl who seemed on the verge of hysterical laughter for no reason that had anything to do with him. Czech kids chattered among themselves in the several packed yet flowing doorways between service bars, dance floors, and toilets. Two anemic, big-boned German girls wrapped in several kinds of leather gurgled observations to one another from a stairwell. And dotting the polyglot crowd of pissed-off, posturing youths were British, Australian, but mostly American speakers of the one language everyone understood at least a little of, English being the language of rock.

Everyone in the crowded vestibule, smoking and tasting flat beers and watery drinks, stared at or stole glances of Luella. She smiled at an Asian girl clad in black chiffon whose accent and vocabulary, which Luella caught a snippet of, as the girl gesticulated to a female comrade likewise adorned, placed her irrefutably in the Ocean Beach section of San Diego. The macabre twins—the other's red hair fanned out over her black shoulders—smiled broadly; both wore retainers, and the sight of silver wire gleaming through black lipstick amused Luella. She felt familial affection, but moved on, knowing that conversation about home with the likes of them would be deadly boring.

"I will fill your cunt with more meat than you've ever dreamed of, missy," an Australian voice like oily sand said to the back of her head. She would not turn; she would not give him the satisfaction of such acknowledgment. "You'll scream with pleasure. I'll make you scream with pleasure." She could feel the heat of his breath on her neck, and smell the beer.

Luella had always trusted her instincts about such situations, and had rarely been wrong. This voice belonged to someone who liked to cause pain. A simple brush-off would be useless. Ignoring would only encourage him.

Were there bouncers? She scanned the room again, moving only her eyes. The Czechs probably couldn't conceive of the necessity, being themselves so civilized even in the throes of Dionysian rapture.

She felt a slight weight on her left hip; he rested his hand there, and then let it fall slowly over the arc of her ass. Apprehension transformed into rage.

"You will remove your hand from my body, or regret having touched me for the remainder of your wretched life," she breathed over her shoulder, keeping her eyes fixed ahead. Then slowly, deliberately, she turned. But no one was there. He had blended back into the somnolent crowd now awaiting the next set.

She exited as the music started up. She was angry with herself for having ventured into such a place that was so thick with pretentions, adolescent posturing, and false passion dovetailed with ennui.

The air had cooled significantly in the brief time since she'd entered the club, and more than anything Luella wanted to revel in being alone. She trotted across the street just ahead of a southbound 12 tram, headed south three blocks, and ascended the serpentine path along the Hunger Wall.

She returned to where the gypsy boy had spent himself upon the grass.

She lay down in the grass near where the boy had released his tensions, his seeds, the code of his existence. She watched a watery-white wisp envelope the three-quarters moon, and release it immediately.

No matter its original purpose, the wall seemed something primal to her. She wondered if every woman didn't have a wall in her heart, a wall that keeps nothing in, nothing out, a wall that divides nothing from nothing, a wall that runs up a hill from the top of which a woman can peer down the length of that useless structure and know that the division it makes is the simple knowledge that desire destroys as it accrues.

A flame engulfed her scalp as she was jerked by her hair into a sitting position. She knew what the chilly blade at her throat would mean. She smelled the beer, and when he spoke clipped commands, first wrapping her blouse around her eyes, she recognized the accent, the voice. How could she have been so stupid not to check if she'd been followed? How, after so many years of avoiding just this in a place where it was common, could it be happening to her in this place where it was not? As he struggled to penetrate her, as his flesh found the entrance to hers, there was a loud rustling in the bushes by the wall; he halted, extracted himself, rose and sprinted thunderously away.

She wiggled her blouse down. He'd cut her panties off of her. She wiped between her legs. Put the useless fabric in her bag, rose, adjusted her skirt. She squinted at the dark wall. Light from the street below glazed it. She shook with rage. Tears ran down her cheeks but she made no sound. She walked slowly, her knees twitching, to the wall.

A cat or bird had scared him off. A weird revulsion at his double cowardice shot through her. Only cowards attack women, especially in the manner he had attacked her, and only the worst kind of coward could be scared away by a cat or a bird. That such a male had entered her even only an inch made her stomach boil, and she threw up on the squat bushes clawing out of the dirt at the base of the wall.

She felt no less violated than if he'd completed the act. She felt no less humiliated. What did he now feel? Surely a man who could be scared by a cat or a bird or a squirrel would feel shame, or was he gloating that he'd entered her an inch, less than an inch?

She touched the wall and remembered the boy, how unabashedly, sincerely, purely even, he had masturbated right where she now stood. It had been like prayer, she now realized, a prayer that the moment might never end, or that ending it might stand for the end of time.

What could change mean to one who prayed that way? How might one such as he improve his life?

All over the planet, boys were praying in fields, over toilets, in their beds, their eyes shut tight. She smiled through her tears, and then she laughed, feeling such affection for that boy and for the pure lusts of all boys everywhere, and then the rage swelled again, and she wanted to destroy the coward who'd humiliated her, whose shallow penetration sullied her as if he'd completed the act. A crime had been committed. But here, she couldn't press. Nikole or Jan would have to translate, suffer each step of the official ordeal with her. And then what? Would local authorities expend resources and time tracking down an Australian rapist of an African/Asian-American woman who'd not even seen his face? How, indeed, would Jan react?

She was in no pain. Anyone gazing upon her now would not find clues of what had happened. She could walk away as though nothing had occurred, take a long bath back at the flat, drink some whiskey, listen to a little Lady Day.

She marched back to the club, got into the face of the boy taking the cover at the door. "*Mluvíte anglicky?*" she asked, barely moving her lips. "Do you remember me leaving here a little while ago?"

"Yes, I do remember." The boy smiled inexplicably. He was skinny and his hair was fizzed out into an artificial 'fro. He looked ridiculous and a little adorable.

"Do you remember anyone following me out, an Australian, maybe?"

"No, I do not remember this, but I remember a group of Australia men who come in. I remember because they were drunk and say in Sidney women are better."

"Are they still in there?"

"Maybe they there still."

Luella started for the door. "*Prominte,* Excuse please," the boy said. "But you must pay!"

Luella turned her eyes upon him for a second, then pushed through the door into the screeching music. She scanned. She patrolled the space, vigilant for English. When she heard it, she asked, "Have you met any Australian men in here tonight? I'm looking for an old Aussie friend." People were kind enough, but no English speaker—an Irish couple, a clutch of Brits, several Americans—had met any Australians, but then she heard two Aussies joking. Neither of them was he, but her heart pounded to hear them.

They were both five-seven or eight. They stood at a tall table, feet crossed at the ankles. They were both balding and sported hilarious comb-overs.

"I'm looking for an Australian man, my height or maybe a little taller. Please don't give me any bullshit. Just tell me where I can find him."

"Now, won't we do, darlin'?" the obviously drunker of the two slurred, and they both laughed.

"Tell me where I can find him," she deadpanned, and the music stopped.

"She's lookin' f'r Danny," the drunker one told the other, who shushed him.

"What do you want with him, sweetheart?" the more focused one inquired. What hair he had was red, and he had a huge, red handlebar.

"Please just tell me where I can find him," she replied a bit more sweetly, hoping that a softer demeanor would elicit the desired response.

"Back at the hotel," the drunker one blurted as he stumbled toward the bar with his empty mug. He had an incomprehensible tattoo across the breadth of his thick neck. Luella thought it might be a Phoenix.

"Which hotel?" She pressed the red mustache, her heart fluttering.

On the street, Luella glanced at a troop of clouds advancing across the moon, and felt the first volley of mist on her face as a gentle late-spring shower glossed the city. She got soaked on the long trek to Wenceslas Square.

The shower quit as she approached the square from Narodní, and when two gypsy men, quite large, one indeed rotund, both dressed in black pants and tacky floral shirts, approached her, she held her bag more tightly to her hip. They asked in German, then English if she wanted to change money; she shook her head and kept walking.

Onto the Square, she observed as she walked a contingent of gypsy women, seven or eight, young, overweight, badly dressed, two holding infants, approach a rather grand looking white-bearded gentleman dressed too formally for the time and place. Luella figured him a rich tourist alley-catting on the Square, and so, obviously, did the women. One hailed him in Italian, another in German, then one toting a baby announced in English, "You are too lonely, Mister!" as they crowded around him. Two of the women had jackets wrapped oddly around their forearms, and one of those two plucked his wallet as the incredulous fellow was getting jostled and propositioned. The deed done, the squad scurried away, and Luella peered into the dark, gorgeous eyes of a placid infant staring over her mother's shoulders as they hustled into the night.

For the first time in over two months, Luella realized she had no idea where she was. She could point to a place on a map. She could fire off some textbook history and news magazine current events. She could recite a dozen or so phrases and recognize by now dozens of words in print. She'd accumulated enough superficial knowledge for perhaps fifty minutes of cocktail party conversation regarding social and cultural differences. Yet she had never felt so utterly American and so utterly lost. From about her third week in Prague until now, she had existed in an unnamed zone between tourist and occupant; the city had acquired a false familiarity which, now ripped away, left her bedazzled.

Did this lend the lie to Nikole's self-righteous ranting about hope, a word that from her European, her central European, her formerly-police-state-monitored mouth had seemed obscene?

Luella Silverlake Jones was striding soaked through a Slavic city in the deepest currents of night, through swarms of gypsies, the only six-foot-plus, Asian-eyed, dark-skinned female within many kilometers, to stare into the cowardly eyes of a man who had harmed her, and she had to admit to herself that if this wasn't hope, nothing was.

The woman at the desk of the small hotel was short and puffy. The deep arcs under her eyes were caked with a skin tone too light for her complexion, and a dark streak ran the path of her part through unnaturally bright-blond hair. Luella asked which room the tall Australian named Danny occupied, and if he was in. The sleepy woman said she could not give out that information.

"He raped me," Luella said dispassionately.

The woman stared up into her eyes, without expression, a long moment. Luella saw a strong life behind the mask of bad makeup and weary, midlife placidity. It had been many years since this person had believed in romantic love, though when she had, she'd believed in it without doubt. Her heart, Luella surmised, had been broken three, perhaps four times. She stared until Luella had to look away, and when she averted her gaze it fell upon a battered English-language paperback. "Passion" was in the title and below the blood-red letters of the title a preternaturally voluptuous blonde, her clothes tattered, was wrapped around the leg of a heartthrob Euro-man who obviously intended to go away.

"Is that any good?" Luella asked, more to break the silence than really to know the woman's opinion.

"He raped you?"

"Yes." What had happened was difficult to describe. "He didn't finish. Something scared him away."

"You are very beautiful."

"Thank you," Luella answered, almost whispering. Her damp clothes were chilling her skin, and she was willing herself not to shiver.

"No, the book is not good. It is only fantasy," the woman said.

"You speak good English."

"I studied at the university. I even taught, but the money was terrible."

"Is he here?"

"Yes, he is here."

"Will you tell me his room number?"

"He is in room three zero one. He's the only one on the floor right now. What will you do?"

"I just want him to see my eyes. He covered my eyes when he raped me."

"How do you know it was he?"

"His voice. I'd heard it before."

"And you just want him to see your eyes?"

"Yes. It's really important."

"I'll go with you. I'll watch." She moved from behind the counter and locked the glass door, turning the sign hanging from the middle bar so it read, Luella assumed, that the hotel was closed.

Luella followed her to the tiny elevator. They were quiet going up. Luella noticed that the woman's dingy knit sweater half-hid a plastic name badge. *Maria.* The cramped lift lurched. A bell rang. Maria glanced through the small window, then opened the door.

Luella knocked. There was a long pause. She turned half her face to Maria, who nodded yes, affirming her earlier assertion that he was there.

"*Kdo je to?*" Danny said through the door.

"Danny McNeal, please open the door," Maria said before Luella could answer.

He was shirtless. His belt was undone. The TV whipped shadowy light around the dim room. He was hairy, rather handsome, with longish straight brown hair that hung in a wave over one eyebrow. He held a liter bottle of the cheapest clear liquor. A cluster of plums was an ugly clot on the white label.

He froze. Then his lips thinned, and he dropped his arms to his sides; he held the half-empty bottle by its neck.

"My name is Luella Silverlake Jones. I am twenty-six-years-old. I am a model, though I have also waited tables, and once I worked in an office. I grew up in Long Beach, California. My father was an E-9, a master chief corpsman in the U.S. Navy, and was much decorated for his service in Vietnam. He's dead." Luella paused. Her expression did not change. Her face, her body didn't move. She seemed not even to breathe. "My mother is a high school math teacher. She's from Japan. She made sure I learned some Japanese as a child. She took me to Sasebo, Japan, four times as I was growing up. My grandparents were ashamed of me but tried to hide their shame. I attended the University of California at Santa Barbara and earned a degree in Communications. I plan to finish graduate school. I love sports, especially track and field. I ran the 400-meter in high school, once coming within two-tenths of a second of the state record. I could have gone to college on a sports scholarship, but chose not to. I've been in love twice." She tilted her head slightly, flicking her eyes down, then back to his. "The first time with a history professor at UCSB, but nothing came of it. I'm now in love with a Czech man named Jan. He's a filmmaker and he's working out of town this week and next. Someday I'd like to have a child." She paused. He didn't move.

"Do you see me, Danny?" she asked. "You see me, don't you? You see a life?"

He didn't move or speak.

"Please answer me. You owe me that much. Look in my eyes and hear my voice. Say yes. Say yes to me."

He didn't slam the door. He receded slowly behind it like something back into its shell. She heard the lock click. "Shit," she breathed.

"What will you do now?" Maria asked.

"Nothing. Go home."

"Are you satisfied?"

"I suppose." Exhaustion permeated her.

"Would you like to hurt him?"

"Not really. I want him to feel humiliated," Luella said.

"Do you think you humiliated him just now?"

"I'm not sure," Luella said as she ducked into the cramped elevator.

"I don't think such a man can be humiliated by a woman," Maria offered, taking Luella aback. "He is one who can deny anything to himself. Even now, he is fixing his mind to fit what happened tonight. His failure to finish with you he is telling himself was pity. And everything you just said is because you desire him. Even now he is certain you sought him out to have sex with him, that you feel rejected by him."

Luella was speechless. They exited the lift.

Maria assumed her position behind the counter. She did not unlock the entrance. Luella asked, "How can you know such things?"

"His eyes. I saw them from a different angle. After the shock of seeing you, he became bored with what you were saying about your life. His eyes glazed over." Maria paused. Did she need to say something that Luella would find painful to hear? "He dismissed you."

"Yes. He dismissed me," Luella agreed, staring off. She was suddenly sleepy, weary and dejected, and the sour odor of her damp clothes filled her head. In his own mind, he couldn't be touched. He was safe from guilt. "He's done it before and he'll do it again," she said.

"Yes, of course," Maria agreed.

"He should be stopped," Luella said.

"Yes," Maria said, "he should be stopped. Use this," she said, pulling a dark gun from her drawer and holding it out to Luella on her palm in one fluid motion.

Luella was shocked, yet reached out and took it. She'd never held a gun.

"The safety is here," Maria pointed, "and there are bullets in it. I found it in a room. It was left by a drug smuggler, a Russian. Danny and his friends smuggle drugs, too, so everyone will think it had to do with drugs. I will say that I saw two men go up there and then come back down quickly. I will say that I heard shots before they came back down. I own this place. Don't worry. Just do it and leave. I will never tell anyone."

Maria was excited. She was, of course, out of her mind, Luella was certain, and yet Luella felt that she could trust this crazy woman. Luella could go up to the third floor, shoot the man who had violated her, would violate other women, and Maria would be her trustworthy accomplice. Her anger swelled, engulfed her weariness. Her eyes filled. She flipped the safety and reentered the lift.

"Come face me again, you fucking coward," she yelled through the door. Maria had taken the stairs, and stood at the elevator, holding the door.

"Piss off," came the bored response.

"Hey, baby, come and get me," she said, softly, holding the pistol with both hands as she'd seen on television. "Yeah, lover, I've got some brown sugar for you. I'm your dream come true. Let me in, baby," she pleaded in her sweetest, sexiest voice. "I want what you've got. I like my men bad. Hurt me, baby. Hurt me all night."

The door opened, then slammed as she shot. She heard howls and curses through the ringing in her ears. She dropped the gun, pushed the door open. The bullet had sliced a bloody ridge in his left cheek, grazing him. Tears washed his eyes. He yelled at her to get the fuck away. He dove for the phone, pressed a pillow to his bleeding face. He dialed the desk, but no one was there to answer. He called Luella a cunt and threw the phone at her.

She calmed, turned, stepped out the door, stooped. She pointed the gun at him and he flinched like an abused child. She missed twice, then grazed his right calf. Then there was only a click, then another, then a bullet skimmed his ass.

He howled like an animal, then, as a child will lose its breath from wailing and its face will contort and freeze into a mask of purest despair-going-to-rage, so did his, and then he caught his breath. He wasn't going to die. No arteries had been struck. He'd be a little disfigured, mostly in hidden places, and the slice on his cheek would become an interesting scar.

Luella wasn't certain how she felt. For a second she was sorry she'd not killed him, then she was immediately relieved. Blood was soaking into the yellow bedspread, and he was moaning and writhing. He was calling her a bitch, a cunt, a niggerbitchcunt, and from his mouth, under those particular circumstances, the epithets smacked vaguely of compliment.

She figured that if Maria were right, that he was a petty drug smuggler, she'd not have to worry about him going to the police. Since he was only nicked and sliced, probably his friends would patch him up, avoid taking him to an emergency room.

She told him in a level voice that if he ever came near her again she'd cut his balls off. But he writhed and moaned with the pillow pressed against his cheek and so covering his ear as his other ear was pressed against the bed, so he likely didn't even register what she'd said. This made her feel a little silly, so she turned, walked out without shutting the door, and took the stairs down to the cramped lobby. Maria was already back behind the counter. Luella told her of his condition, and the bitter, no-doubt slightly crazy Czech lifted her eyes from the book and shrugged.

"Just throw it in the river," she said without emotion. Luella stuffed the little weapon in her large leather purse, dragged the black bag off the counter, adjusting the strap on her shoulder. "It'll be quite a mess up there," she said.

"I will turn the mattress over and throw away the sheets," Maria responded, but Luella had been speaking more figuratively, referring to when Danny's colleagues would return. Certainly he and the others would confront Maria. But Maria had indeed understood what Luella had meant and, after a pause, smiled and simply said, with such calm conviction that Luella did not doubt her, "They will not dare say anything to me," and Luella realized there was more to Maria, her sleazy little hotel and its drug-smuggling clientele than was at first obvious.

She glanced both ways; pedestrian traffic trickled across the Charles Bridge, but at two in the morning most traversers looked, at best, dazed. The air was clean from the rain, and tepid breezes were perfect. She slipped the gun from her bag and dropped it over the edge. A black-stone saint seemed to stare past her; the Charles Bridge was flanked on both sides by very pious black-stone effigies of larger-than-life men.

She turned and gave her weight to the thick railing, crossed her feet at the ankles, adjusted the purse strap on her shoulder, and watched the people stride or stumble by.

A dark boy stopped ten feet away. Gypsy? She couldn't tell. He dressed expensive Italian from shirt to shoes, but he was too dark to be Italian. He stared at her. He was thin and sinewy, and his eyes were large, dark and liquid, his mouth sensual.

He smiled at her, staring directly and deeply into her eyes, and she was tempted.

Interviews in Prague

2009

Since Mirek's mother owned the building in Prague 5, and since the space had once contained a kind of proletarian cafeteria and so was already configured for food service, Sandy was fairly certain that she and Mirek could transform the space into the high-end fine-dining establishment she'd always dreamed of running.

Mirek purchased the entire kitchen—stoves, refrigerators, grills, deep fryers, counters, pots and pans, even tongs—from a Bulgarian wholesaler, had it shipped by rail, transported from the train in three loads by a nasty, bilge-belching Soviet-era truck. As the workmen wrestled the items into what would be the kitchen, Sandy despaired; it was shitty equipment. She didn't even have to inspect it closely. Inferiority wafted from the lot of it.

"Motherfucker, you promised me high end. This kitchen is bullshit."

"What we save on the kitchen, we'll be able to pour into the dining room. No one cares what the kitchen looks like."

"I don't care how it looks, douchebag. I need even, reliable heat. I need to know that the goddamned refrigeration won't go out overnight and spoil everything. I need the peace of mind that good, reliable equipment offers. Bulgaria? Are you kidding me? This stuff was built in Bulgaria?"

"It was built in Russia. I bought it from a Bulgarian," Mirek corrected.

His father spirited him out of Czechoslovakia in '86, when Mirek was three. His father, trained as a civil engineer, had also been a poet of some standing. Josef Bílek garnered employment at Louisiana Technical University with a split appointment between the math and literature departments. Having left his wife without divorcing her, he could not marry the woman who became Mirek's American mom, though that had been a minor point until Josef Bílek's massive and fatal heart attack in '98. At the age of fifteen, most of his mother tongue but a trace memory, Mirek had returned to Prague and to a mother he did not know.

Sandy sighed. She would make due. She would upgrade everything piecemeal. She would take deep breaths and simply deal with this boy-man's incompetence. She would take the long view. She'd met him in an Irish pub near Old Town Square. He'd been intrigued by the fact that she'd received her culinary training in New Orleans, that she was a New Orleans girl through and through. He'd told her stories about his many visits to New Orleans as a child and adolescent; indeed, New Orleans had been his "city," the big city nearest his rinky-dink college town. Their conversation in a bar had taken flight. They'd had good sex, and he'd started talking about his mother's restituted properties, how she'd received three buildings from the new democratic state in the early nineties, and how she had sold two of them to acquire the funds to refurbish the most valuable of the three. Promises had been made. A two-week vacation in a country to which she had vague, three-generations-removed ata-vistic connections got extended, and then Sandy left a good life in post-storm New Orleans, as a sous chef at Commander's Palace, to run her own operation in an ancient, beautiful city. If the whole thing went south, she'd told herself, she could always go back; even failure in so sexy and exotic a place as Prague would look good on her résumé.

"Okay, son," she began, "you don't make a single other unilateral decision. Is that clear? You and I are going to sit down with your mama. I need to work with her directly. I need to communicate with her directly. Is that clear?"

"My mother doesn't speak a word of English."

"Then you'll interpret."

"I'm not too hot at that," Mirek confessed. He was more or less fluent, though native-speaking Czechs often had a difficult time understanding him. Even his mother had to ask him to repeat things.

"What she and I have to talk about is pretty basic," Sandy concluded. They were no longer lovers, and Sandy was all business.

Over the coming days, she would conduct interviews for both the kitchen and the wait staff. Two of her buddies, a terrific waiter and a solid line cook from Commanders, had vowed to arrive within the next three to five weeks, but they would be of limited value if she were not able to find reliable English-speaking Czechs. She supposed that Mirek could serve as a maître d', but she needed him to be the business guy, the person dealing with city ordinances, taxes, and other such stuff. She especially needed him for buying and selling, but primarily for keeping his mama's money rolling in. She needed him to do exactly what she fucking told him to do.

She'd been happy to discover that fresh seafood was shipped in daily from Paris, and she and Mirek had fashioned a deal that would deliver product to the restaurant four days a week. Striking deals for produce and high-grade beef had proved simple enough, though beef was pricier than she'd anticipated. Sandy's Cajun Kitchen had a nice ring, though *Sandy Cajunská Kuchyně* didn't, at least not to her ear.

Her office was furnished entirely from Ikea, so seemed to her a sterile geometry of mere function. Her first interview was scheduled for 2 p.m., arrived at 2:40 and did not apologize. She was a mousy blonde who seemed to think that volume compensated for the halting nature of her English. Sandy got rid of her quickly. Her four o'clock arrived on time. He had a dozen silver rings lined up in the ridge of each ear and a large ring in his septum, but his English was strong and he smiled fetchingly. Had he ever worked in food service? He'd helped his grandfather slaughter and roast a pig each mid-June family gathering. Had he ever had any paying job? He had once been paid to staple to poles and walls flyers advertising a local rock band. Had he ever cooked anything but the annual pig? His babička lived with his family, and cooked everything. He'd not even been allowed in the kitchen. Was he in college? He was studying American literature, specifically literature about the Wild West. He would graduate in a year, and be eminently unemployable. Was he willing to work four ten-hour shifts a week? Sure. He would start out at a hundred crowns an hour. More than five bucks an hour. His eyes got big.

"So much?"

"And tips."

"What is that?"

"Gratuity."

"What is that?"

"It's when the customer leaves money on the table for service." He would definitely be on the floor. He was cute and disarmingly self-effacing, and not someone she'd want to work with in the kitchen. She'd end up killing him. "In the States, fifteen percent is the norm."

At this he giggled. "No Czech would leave so much."

"Yeah, I know, but I'm hoping to attract a lot of expats, and most Czechs will leave something."

"This will be a very good job!" Květa Kola enthused.

Her five o'clock was an immaculately groomed man in his mid to late-fifties. He wore a black suit he'd owned probably for two decades and kept in excellent condition. His black tie was in a perfect Windsor. He presented Sandy his résumé. She leafed through it.

"You were headwaiter at Allium in the Four Seasons in Chicago. I've met Kevin Hickey, the executive chef. Terrific, talented guy."

"Yes, we stay in touch."

"You've worked in a half dozen very good establishments."

"Thank you."

"Why in God's name are you here?" He had silver at his temples, and it was appealing. He was swarthier than most Czechs. Was he Roma?

He paused, stared briefly over her shoulder. "Love brought me home," he said.

Sandy was speechless for a few seconds. "How long will you stay here?"

"Until I die."

"I mean here, at this restaurant."

"I assumed as much. I will stay until I die, or until you close this establishment."

He was slim, though possessed a broad frame. His face was filled with a contented sorrow. "Will you serve as my maître d'?"

"I will serve as I am needed."

"Will you help me train the waitstaff?"

"I will train them."

"I can start you out at seven thousand a week. It's not what you're used to, but your salary will grow with the business."

"In this economy, seven thousand crowns is generous."

"For the first six months or so, you'll be expected to work six ten-hour days each week."

"At least." He was placid, resigned, coolly committed. She trusted him but wasn't sure why.

She sat back her plastic swivel chair. "We're going to be spending a lot of time together," she glanced at his résumé, "Milan. May I call you Milan?"

"Of course."

She explained her relationship with Mirek, was frank though cautious regarding her assessment of Mirek's judgment. She explained her own work history and ambitions. She explained the restaurant's concept and her own timeline of goals. It was his turn. He stared down a moment, gathered himself, and took two deep breaths.

His résumé indicated that he'd trained in Milan and in New York. The attached letters of recommendation on letterhead from each of the six U.S. establishments where he'd worked heaped unconditional praise upon him. He was tenfold too qualified for this gig. "I grew up in Slapy, a few minutes outside of Prague. My father was a dissident, signed Charter 77, so university study was not available to me in the '70s. I worked in pubs and horrible communist restaurants. I got out in my late twenties, landed in Milan, learned Italian, attended culinary school."

"You never wanted to work in kitchens?"

"I started in a kitchen, but felt more comfortable on the floor. But, as you know, every good waiter should receive culinary training."

"Hallelujah! But that's just a dream."

"Be that as it may . . ." his voice trailed. Sandy wanted to hear about the love part, and Milan knew it. "I shall cut to the proverbial chase." He straightened his spine. "Before I . . . 'escaped' is too melodramatic. Before I snuck out of Czechoslovakia—and actually surprisingly little stealth was required—I'd impregnated a beautiful girl and was unaware for many years that I had a child. That beautiful girl died of alcohol and bitterness perhaps a decade after, leaving our daughter to be raised by her witless, vindictive grandmother. My daughter gave birth seven years ago to her own daughter, and left the child to the state. My partner, Rafael, and I are raising the child. She is a treasure. She is the love for which I have returned."

"Do you have a green card?" she asked.

"Yes, after much red tape and frustration."

"Rafael?"

"He is married to a lovely woman in Chicago, and, yes, possesses a green card. He's a computer wiz, can find employment anywhere, works mostly at home."

"Will you eventually take your granddaughter back to the States?"

"Green card status does not extend to grandchildren born abroad. The bureaucracy would take years to negotiate." He retrieved his wallet from his back pocket. The child was as dark as he; her black hair cascaded in curls to her shoulders. The photo seemed a kind of kiddy mug shot. Her lovely little face was unsmiling and stared directly into the camera.

"She's a beauty, Milan." She paused. "Was it odd to be named Milan when you studied in Milan?" It was a stupid question. "That's a stupid question. I'm sorry. What's her name?"

"Bella. She's in second grade. She's very bright."

"You seem quite fit. But raising such a young child at your age must be a little scary." She paused. "You'll have to get used to my frankness, Milan." She smiled weakly.

"Rafael is thirty-five. He adores Bella. I have no worries," he said, and for the first time a wan smile formed on his mouth. "Do you have children?" The interview became a conversation.

"No, I'd rather stick a six-inch spike in my eye than get pregnant," she said. "I like kids, just don't want any."

"Perhaps you'll change your mind," he said perfunctorily.

"I may change my mind about climate change and the war on drugs, but it's highly unlikely. Kids? Never."

"Have you ever been in love?"

Sandy was startled by the question, but answered as honestly as she could, "I don't know. Probably not."

"Did you come to Prague looking for love?"

"Maybe."

"Do you love your work?"

"Adore it."

"How good are you?"

"Very, very good."

"Are you close to your parents?" He seemed genuinely interested.

"I'm very close to my father. He's a basketball coach at Brother Martin, though that won't mean anything to you. My mother is an English professor at Loyola. We're not that close but I admire her."

"You grew up Catholic," he stated with assurance.

"Yeah," she confirmed.

"Do you still believe?"

"Never did, really. But once the Church gets its fucking hooks in you . . ."

"I know."

"I go into cathedrals here," she said, as in a dream. "My favorite is Loreto, behind the Castle. It's dedicated entirely to Mary."

"Are you comforted in Prague by cathedrals? Do they seem holy?"

"I'm comforted, in a way. But they seem like museums. Well, Loreto doesn't seem like a museum. I feel female power there. But the only other holy places I've ever known have been restaurants. Not all, Lord knows, but the good ones. The really good ones are holy places."

"And what is a holy place?" His brow was furrowed. He awaited her answer with deep sincerity.

"I think it's something between a hospital emergency room and a chapel. It is a place of intensive care outside of time. The patrons come to be outside of time and to be attended to. The best waiters are angels. They anticipate need and desire. They are unobtrusive. They are graceful and formal."

"I am an angel?"

"If you're as good as your résumé says you are. If you're as good as I bet you are."

"What are you? Are you an angel? Are your cooks angels?" There was only a hint of whimsy in his voice.

She was silent a moment. "Chefs are demigods, their cooks divine acolytes." She laughed a little. This good man would be an excellent partner. The timing between the kitchen and the floor would be almost perfect.

"Do you pray?" Oddly, the question seemed to be changing the subject.

"When I cook." Was *she* passing the interview?

"That's too easy an answer," he shot back.

She glanced at the ceiling. It was cracked and dingy. The whole place needed to be stripped and painted. "Sometimes, desperately and without words."

He seemed satisfied with the answer, rose, as did she, and they shook hands like two people who had done good business.

Deep Sorrow on the Face,
Light Laughter in the Heart

1999

Dear Reader (my phantom interlocutor; the sibling I never had, the mother, the father I lost; representative of my bloodline's hosts who perished; you for whom the voice in my head holds forth; constituency of my soul; that to which I cannot lie even as I lie to myself):

The last time Hitler sat on a toilet, he did so in contempt of his own despair. I imagine him sober, on a bunker commode, khaki trousers around his ankles, simultaneously mourning his beloved half-niece Geli and thinking through the details of suicide. He will finish, marry Eva in the spirit of wiping, and join his beloved Geli on the void. I've read that Hitler was enamored of feces, and that Geli and/or Eva shat often on his chest to his utter delight. I, frankly, don't think the guy was nearly that interesting.

The victim of occasional sobriety, I arrived in Prague on the 20th of April 1994. I'd procured a considerable sum ripping off the most powerful coke dealer in Chula Vista, California, as well as my lover, and heard that Prague was cool, but also recalled my Aunt Gertrude reading me a story of Rabbi Loew and his mighty golem, a monster made of river clay that protected the Jews of Prague. I had to go somewhere or die a horrible death, so I parked my money where I could access it electronically, and flew. The money I ripped off will probably last until I am in my mid-fifties, at which time I will have no *curriculum vitae* by which to garner gainful employment, no employment history at all beyond the age of nineteen when I began dealing. Possessing no marketable skills, I shall enter my gray years fucked. But for now, in Prague, I live comfortably if modestly.

I'm not certain why I spend so much of my free time—all of my time is free; I do little more than lounge—speculating upon the final hours of Hitler's consciousness. I do not speak German and have small knowledge of history beyond that of most moderately well-read nonacademicians. And yet I feel a connection. Hitler is Elmer Fudd. Human decency, in all its ironic shit, is da wabbit, who always wins. Alas, I want to be da wabbit, but awaken each morning with a strong compulsion to stalk human decency. "Kill da wabbit. Kill da wabbit . . ."

It is 1999, April whatever. I am thirty-seven-years-old. I graduated from San Diego State University with a BA in Something. I am on a budget, and over the past five years have practiced extraordinary fiscal prudence, living on an average of $35,000 a year. The average Czech salary is under ten grand annually, but the average Czech doesn't eat out twice a day and traverse the continent a half dozen times a year, including Alpine ski excursions. Budgets are relative to need, and need is relative to character, of which I am woefully deficient. I calculate that, at my current rate of consumption, I will be destitute in the third or fourth month of 2014, or thereabouts (I'm not clever enough to calculate for inflation and fluctuating currency exchange rates). I'll not bore you, Reader, with the math. Nor shall I bore you with the Byzantine particulars of legal residency in the Czech Republic, a condition to which I've not even bothered to aspire.

That I have resources is born of the fact that Julio informed me that if I did not insert my penis into his hound's vagina (she was a fetching Basset), he would blow my best friend's brains out. My best friend was my lover, Maggie, and I could not allow that horrible human being to end her life. So I imagined the young Catherine Deneuve. I imagined the young Brigitte Bardot. I imagined Madonna. I imagined Susan Sarandon. I imagined all of them naked and randy, but I couldn't sustain the fantasy of any of those beautiful women, and so I couldn't fuck Julio's comely Basset, but, in a moment of genius—and please understand, Reader, that I know I am not a genius, but that genius is sometimes visited upon individuals in desperate circumstances—I lifted that lovely hound and in one sweeping motion heaved her toward Julio's face.

Julio shot his beloved pet with a sawed-off shotgun he'd been aiming in Maggie's general direction. The dog's blood changed the room into an installation piece. I grabbed a letter opener and thrust it to the hilt into Julio's thigh. He howled like a punk. I dragged Maggie's hand and we escaped. Maggie married her second cousin in '96 and lives in Tucson. I ripped her off for her investment, but, having saved her life, did not and do not feel remorse. The deal was that Julio would put up half and she, my financer, the other. Good is relative.

Which is to say that Julio found out where I'd flown to and dispatched his baby sister, a homicidal maniac who is referred to on the streets of Chula Vista and Imperial Beach as *la Hoja Dama*, the Blade Lady. Her charge, reported Fast Freddy on the phone last night, is to transport my severed balls back to Chula Vista.

Reader, I have numerous friends within the expatriate network of Prague; I have some Czech acquaintances, two Czech friends, but I am primarily a creature of the expat community, a collection of mostly twenty and thirty-somethings who fled banality only to witness its inexorable blossoming in this ancient place. My best friend is Wanda, a lipstick lesbian from L.A. who married a Czech whom she holds in utter, though loving, contempt. Her lover is her husband's sister, Ludmila, whom everyone calls Roxanne. The three own a bookstore/café called the Old Globe, an expat oasis of English-language used and new books and magazines, as well as authentic American breakfasts and burgers.

"How do you know she's here?" Wanda asked.

"My boy Freddy called me last night."

"Fast Freddy from I.B.?" Wanda and I met at the Chart House in Coronado. She was down from L.A. with a girl who was an assistant manager of the restaurant. Wanda slung cocktails there four nights a week.

"The same."

"Why would he bother?"

I'd finished my eggs, stubbed my cigarette out in some residual yoke. "Partly because the Blade Lady burned him on a small deal. Partly, I think, because he's tired of being humiliated by Julio."

"Whatcha gonna do?" Wanda seemed more curious than alarmed. That she is my best friend is sometimes disheartening.

Adolf Hitler, Reader, had intimacy issues, especially towards the end when he feared that just about anyone he knew could kill him at almost any time. He was of course paranoid and delusional, coked up much of the time, but who knows how many subordinates, even cooks and maids, fantasized offing the little prick? Those final couple of years his personal assistants must have hated their jobs. A doctor, I read somewhere, was executed for suggesting that Hitler had mental health issues, though I'm not sure if "mental health issues" was the phrase I read; I'm not even certain that I actually read such an anecdote, heard it in a documentary, or dreamed it. Aunt Gertrude read the same story to me night after night of the entire summer of my eighth year, and I never questioned the redundancy, never complained. The golem I pictured as a giant version of the Fantastic Four's Thing. I considered him "our" Thing, a Jewish Thing who, unfortunately, didn't, or couldn't, crack wise.

"She just checked into the Continental," I said, kissed Wanda on the cheek, walked out into a lovely spring day, *The Prague Post* folded into my armpit.

I am in a Profit Taxi because it is the only kind that doesn't routinely rip off Americans. I'm going to fuck up Julio's demented sister before she has a chance to cut my throat and then my scrotum. She is small but wiry and preternaturally strong. The first time I had sex with her I was overwhelmed by her physical strength. She assumed positions in which she held my entire weight as well as her own with one arm. I don't think I could win a fair fight with her, but have no intention of fighting her, fairly or otherwise. I'm simply going to shoot her in her feet.

I have shot seven people in their feet (near the toes). In Coronado, I am famous as the drug dealer who would not kill you for ripping him off, but who would not hesitate to blow a hole in your foot. One fellow, a brain-dead surfer, I shot in both his sandy feet at dusk on the Coronado beach near the North Island Air Base fence.

I purchased my American Eagle Luger from the American vice-president of a British-owned holding company. He was a drinking buddy for a while, and loved my stories of dealing drugs in southern California. Eventually, I ran out of stories, and he had few of much interest, so we drifted apart, but before we disengaged he gave me a great deal on the pistol.

I have never been arrested. I have shot seven people in their feet, including the surfer who was a special case. I have purchased and sold many kilos of weed and cocaine, have burned through a couple million dollars not including the piles I took from Julio and Maggie. All in all, my career as a third-tier drug dealer was successful by any objective measure. I smoked very little pot, snorted coke only occasionally, and then simply not to alarm my business partners and customers. I would not have had to rip off Julio and Maggie had I not purchased Aunt Gertrude a condo near Old Town. She is eighty-three and judges me a bad Jew. She thinks "the anonymous source" that purchased her condo was a goy lover from her youth who left it to her in his will. She loves Oprah, and takes healthful walks through Old Town every day, wearing a comically huge straw hat and owlish sunglasses. She is a good Jew to the extent that she keeps kosher and attends a conservative synagogue. Because I am her only living relative, other Jewish families have adopted her, so she gets to attend many weddings and funerals. She is definitely da wabbit.

Reader, Julio and his sister are evil, which means hurting and killing are thrilling to them. They are from San Salvador, where the siblings participated in death squads in the late '70s. Once, drunk and coked up, Julio claimed that it had been he who murdered Archbishop Romero, but that assertion, I'm certain, was mere bluster. On the eight occasions I visited his domain, either *Scar Face* or *Reservoir Dogs* was loaded into the VCR of his enormous television, as though on a loop, and with the sound off.

The Continental does not have cameras above the Lobby Level, which is really quite stupid but fortunate for me. In this pinstriped suit, wearing this blue tie and these sensible black loafers, I will be as incognito as wallpaper. Hitler suffered from numerous ailments, real and imagined, not the least of which was a very real case of Parkinson's. As a Jew, I suffer, Reader, from the knowledge of human suffering. In this, I am, like every other Jew, a meta-Jew. I loved it when Bugs looked right at me before or after confounding Elmer. Sometimes he just looked, and the eye contact said it all; sometimes he cracked wise.

There she is, eating Svíčková in the main restaurant of the hotel. She looks jetlagged and will not recognize me, on her periphery, suited up, trimmed and beardless. I'm sure her plan is to go back to bed, rise early and begin to hunt me. She knows that as an avid if casual reader, I probably hang out at English language bookstores. Tomorrow, if she hasn't already, she will peruse *The Prague Post* and see the running ad for the Old Globe. But it doesn't matter, because I will shoot her in her feet tonight.

I am slightly behind her, about ten meters away sipping a double shot of Slivovice at the bar, chasing it with Mattoni. After I shoot the Blade Lady in her feet, I will take a late bus to Karlovy Vary, my favorite place on the planet. Tomorrow I shall stroll among the lovely fountains, sipping the various waters from my porcelain Karlovy-Vary-sipping-thing. I will get a full body massage. I will try to find an English-speaking daughter of rich Russians to screw.

The present tense is always a lie. As Hitler, himself very likely of Jewish descent, sits on the toilet, he recalls his young niece, not a smart or interesting girl, but all the same the only person in whose company he could relax into himself. She did not defecate on his chest and never was it suggested that she do so, but he recalls being surprised by one of her unflushed turds sprawled on the turd-inspection ridge of a typical central European toilet, and being inexplicably moved by the sight. As he relieves himself, he knows that this is the final time he will perform this biological act. Reader, he is, even as he evacuates, nostalgic for toilets, nostalgic for emptying his bowels. Aunt Gertrude insisted that I piss sitting down so as to keep the area around the toilet clean. It was 1968; my parents had gone down in a DC 10 from Salt Lake City back to San Diego a few months previously; she took me in and tried to teach me how to be a proper Jew. Into my early teens, I assumed that all Jewish men sat down to piss.

As she rises, I face the bar. She passes. I rise. Five loud Germans crowd the elevator. She is behind them; I am in front. When she nudges forward at the third floor I turn away slightly, then follow her off. When she knew me, my hair flowed over my shoulders. Now it is as short as a banker's, and I've lightened it with product. When she knew me, I had a moustache and beard. When she arrives at her room I grip the Lugar and shove her hard through the door as she unlocks it, press my back against the door and flip on the light. She glares up at me from the carpet; recognition cascades over her face, and she laughs. She kicks off her shoes. grabs her knees. She is making it easy.

I rip the phone from the wall, shoot her in her right foot, then her left. She doesn't scream, but gasps after each shot. She knew it was coming as soon as she recognized me. I grab her purse from the floor as a kind of favor. She is wearing a sensible gray pantsuit. Her Samsonite is opened on her king-size bed. She is creepy in her serenity.

In the hall, a little girl, six, maybe, is dressed for the pool; pink float devices ring her arms; her one-piece is pink and seahorses frolic all over it. Her hefty mama wears a white terry cloth robe over her swimsuit. They chatter in Italian. Surely they heard the shots, but Mama is persuaded that it was a backfire, or from a television. I smile at the little one. She stares at the gold lamé clutch I hold like something I've forgotten I'm transporting. The Luger is uncomfortably in the waistband of my pants. I feel as though it may slip into my pants and down my pant leg. If that occurs, I will have to stop walking and look very clumsy holding the gun, under the fabric, against my crotch, thigh, or knee. I will have to work it down my pant leg and lift it from my pant cuff.

I breeze through the lobby, holding the gold clutch against the Luger that is hidden by my coat. I find a taxi; it is not Profit, but it will do under the circumstances. She will tell an English-speaking assistant manager that a blond-haired, blue-eyed fellow wearing jeans and a T-shirt shot her and stole her purse. I dig through her purse, and, as I thought, her passport is not there. It is no doubt at the hotel desk. They'll stanch her wounds, get her to an emergency room. She'll enter the plane on crutches or in a wheel chair. If Julio were smart, and though he is cunning in the trade he is exceedingly stupid, he would hire local talent, Ukrainians, probably, for a hell of a lot cheaper than it was for a round-trip ticket from San Diego and a room at the Continental. He could easily have purchased such services with a few telephone calls. But he literally wants my balls, to hold a sandwich baggie up to the light and examine them closely. It is a primary feature of evil to overreach, to seek operatic moments of triumph and thereby insure its own defeat.

Julio, the number one drug dealer in Chula Vista, dear Reader, ripped off the number one dealer in San Diego—picture a Chihuahua stealing a pit bull's squeaky toy—who happened also to be the leader of either the Crips or the Bloods, I wasn't at the time sure which; I was the biggest drug dealer in Coronado, and some of my business spilled into La Jolla. My clients were the children of wealth, and, occasionally, their parents. Gangs never concerned me, were never an issue, until I partnered, for a single score, with Julio. Because he had ripped off the number one dealer in San Diego (a Blood, as it turned out), he implored me to make the deal; he put up $300,000, and Maggie fronted me the same.

His desire to humiliate me, his willingness to discomfort his beloved dog in the process, was in part born of his discovering that I'd been having sex with his baby sister, but more to the point that I'd brought multiple kilos of baby powder to his Chula Vista bungalow. Maggie was furious that I'd been banging the Blade Lady, who'd gotten out of prison on parole a couple of months earlier, but Maggie is nothing if not all business, and had fronted me the money for the faux cocaine. Heavily invested in Coronado real estate and divorced from a cheating heart surgeon, Maggie was liquid. Her second cousin in Tucson scored.

Why didn't I taste one of the kilos? Why did I even bother delivering the shit to Julio? Regarding the former question: cowardice. Regarding the second: Maggie, as his co-investor, remained with Julio awaiting my return, which is to say that she was his hostage. If I'd tasted the shit and bugged out, he'd have killed her. I'd not have had the courage to return to his bungalow, even with a gun.

There is footage of Czechs crowded on Wenceslas Square, more than a hundred thousand of them, giving the Nazi salute to troop transports. As they saluted, some sang the Czechoslovak national anthem, "Where Is My Home?" Perhaps only a people whose sense of national identity is tethered to an interrogative could spontaneously make such a gesture of supreme irony. It was their charming though pathetic way of giving the finger to the Nazis.

At the Romania Hotel in Karlovy Vary, the rooms are small though clean, and there is no CNN. I shall go to sleep to the sound of gently rushing water, and awaken to it. There are trees there four, five hundred years old. If the springs happen not to possess therapeutic value, at least the strolling between and drinking of them are a balm to the soul. My mother was a famous poet, my father a proctologist and her biggest fan. They were returning from the University of Utah where Mom had given a reading from a new collection of poems. Aunt Gertrude didn't think much of her sister's poetry, didn't think it was Jewish enough. Alas, neither parent had life insurance and died gloriously in debt.

One of my two Czech friends, Filip, a twenty-something dealer whom I mentor from time to time, once sighed, as we twirled our snifters, tabled on the deck of the ridiculous *Botel*, gazing into the Vltava, "*Light laughter on the face, deep sorrow in the heart*." He said it in Czech, and I understood *srdce*, heart, and laughter, face and sorrow registered, but of course I couldn't put it all together grammatically. Barely ten million people speak Czech, and a growing percentage of them speaks English. Their greatest writer, Milan Kundera, has become a fucking Frenchman.

But their genius is the reversal of that adage. I love them for reversing it, in their hearts. Heil Hitler, but where's my home? It's here, motherfucker, in my heart.

Where is *my* home?

Julio and Maggie paid a considerable sum, Reader, for twelve kilograms of baby powder. Sex with Julio's baby sister was rewarding, on two or three levels, though, finally, boring. Sex and contempt are not oil and water, though the viscosity of the former slows absorption of the latter. My nut with her was incredible, circus incredible, high-wire incredible, netless trapeze incredible, but a boring kind of incredible. Like porn. Like shitting in despair. Skin, gut, clean, cook, and then eat the fucking rabbit. Good is not relative.

I want to crawl into the golem's asshole. I want to occupy its bowels. At my Bar Mitzvah, Uncle Charley got so drunk he drowned in puke. He was a merchant marine, and I discovered a couple of years later that he'd been a casual scholar of the Talmud, that on all of those long crossings he'd studied it and many books about it. Uncle Charley had never exhibited, to my prepubescent regard, a particular interest in justice. Though once, as we watched the Vikings edge out the Chargers, he blamed the loss on poor officiating. His solace, as I recall, was that at least the Chargers beat the spread.

I read somewhere that Hitler consulted his bunker SS doc as to the most reliable method of suicide and was told that a combination of cyanide and gunshot to the head would be most effective. I imagine him hunched there on the toilet, elbows on his bare knees, thinking through the logistics. How long after biting down on the capsule should he pull the trigger? Why would the pill even be necessary? Should he put the gun in his mouth or to his temple? For that fleeting moment of grotesque practicality, did he become da wabbit?

She never told me her given name. She said that when we were together I should simply call her Puta, but that if I ever slipped and called her by that name in the company of others she'd murder me. Her four-room house in Imperial Beach was a ghastly purple. A pit bull puppy had rendered her tiny yard of dirt a disgusting minefield.

The sex was epic and ridiculous. The puppy howled as she came, and she rose from the shadows of our bodies and walked determinedly from the spunk of our sex into the dim glow of her kitchen. A drawer opened.

I rose from her mattress onto my elbow. A light snapped on; the window above my head glowed. I parted the mangled blinds as though I were a dentist, and saw her squeeze that puppy against her naked breasts and run a knife across its throat. Love the rabbit.

Because he owed me eight thousand dollars and did not wish to be shot in both of his sandy feet again, my surfer client limped onto the city bus lugging a duffle bag filled with forty thousand mediocre facsimiles of twenty-dollar bills. A confederate of the number one drug dealer in San Diego would enter the bus at the first stop on the other side of the Coronado Bridge. As my surfer—dumb as a box of rocks, wearing swimming trunks and a Hawaiian shirt unbuttoned, long blond hair bleached white by the sun, blue-eyed and so deeply tanned he will surely one day sport numerous melanomas—padded barefoot up the steps of the bus, needing to use the rail like an old person to compensate for his wounded, recently unbandaged feet, I felt like a father seeing his boy off to school. Reader, you may not believe me, but that is how I felt. The little Aryan bastard had ripped me off for thirteen thousand dollars, still owed me eight, but vapidity so lofty as his on occasion touches the sublime: to my question once as to his future plans, he smiled broadly and declared that he would study to become a pharmacy.

Seated on a nearly empty bus, he gave me a shy, boyish wave as the bus pulled from the curb and turned onto Fourth Avenue. He would return with a backpack filled with kilos of baby powder he'd exchanged for the duffle bag of forty thousand mediocre counterfeit twenties I'd purchased for a mere three thousand bucks from a retired chief petty officer. Luckily, the number one drug dealer in San Diego sent someone as stupid as my surfer to make the exchange. I'd stashed Julio's and Maggie's money, and when I arrived at Julio's Chula Vista bungalow and he sampled the shit I'd brought him, he ordered me to screw his pooch.

I extract the overnight bag I'd stashed earlier in a station locker. Having already liberated eighteen thousand crowns, roughly seven hundred bucks, from the Blade Lady's purse, I toss the little gold pouch, return ticket and all, into the trash. But then I reach into the can and pluck her California driver's license from its gaping mouth.

She is Isabelle Alegria. She is five feet three inches and weighs one hundred and twenty-eight pounds (all muscle). She stares not into the camera, but over it. She is beautiful and brutal beyond understanding. Mine, anyway. At the Terezín museum, located in what was once the Nazis "show" camp, the one the Nazis invited the Swiss Red Cross to inspect, and from which almost everyone was subsequently transported to Auschwitz, there are, under glass, pictures drawn by the community's children. Most are excruciatingly cheerful. I will not, dear Reader, presume to describe one to you. Doing so would be disgusting.

I am snug inside the golem's rectum, this bus to beautiful Karlovy Vary. The golem is not da wabbit; he is merely a mighty receptacle. Rabbi Loew, his spirit, is da wabbit. The children of Terezín were little bunnies, soft and cuddly and doomed. It is for them that Bugs and I looked conspiratorially into each other's eyes, though I only know that now.

My dear, imaginary reader, occupant of a chair in a modest space on the twilit outskirts of doom, read this shard of my life and judge not my life or its telling, for what is written on my heart is legible only to the dead. What is written here I scratch into the dry bowels of the golem.

Bag

2001

The obese Roma heaved a duffel bag into the jagged hedgerow and waddled up the steep hill of Sinkulova. A black Škoda rolled parallel to the fat man; the passenger shouted out the window in a Slavic tongue neither Czech nor Slovak. Two men jumped from the boxy car. They wore dark leisure suits and Elvis sideburns. They screeched in tandem and beat the swarthy fellow with what looked like billy clubs. His greasy black hair, down to his shoulders, filled with blood and he fell on his ass crossing his forearms in front of his face, weeping and pleading. They lifted him by his armpits and wedged him into the back seat of the Škoda, then sped away.

It was 8:23 Sunday morning. Blake was returning from the clubs: dancing with hookers, 7 a.m. breakfast at McDonald's. His buddy Markey had jumped off the Charles Bridge, and miraculously survived only to get arrested, though was quickly let go with a citation Markey would never pay given that he was returning home for good on Wednesday.

Blake assumed the unlucky fellow was Roma, though he could have been anything swarthy. It was however most likely that in Prague, in early September, 2001, such a fellow, dressed motley in red corduroy pants and a multicolored T-shirt whose horizontal strips only enhanced his considerable girth, would be gypsy.

Blake rose from a crouch behind a lamppost, dropped his arms to his sides, stared. He could see the blood on the cement in the next block, forty or so meters away. He turned and ran down Sinkulova, toward the Vltava, but veered, took the steep cement steps up to Vyšehrad. The sirens were faint but approaching, and he did not wish to bear witness. He didn't speak Czech beyond restaurant and taxi, and recounting the incident through an interpreter would be tedious.

He cut through the park, across the lawn between the ten-meter tall statues flanking the green. Desiring more respite than sanctuary, he tried the great doors of St. Peter and Paul Cathedral, half knowing they would not be unlocked so early. The sirens, a quarter mile away, a hundred meters or more below the rise of Vyšehrad, ceased, Blake assumed, upon their arrival to the scene. He imagined neighbors in robes mulling around the bloodstain, bearing witness as best they could.

Drugs? Vendetta? People, as a rule, didn't get beaten and hauled away on Prague streets. Crimes of stealth were the norm: pickpockets on the Metro, purse and camera thieves plucking from the backs of tourists' restaurant chairs, connoisseurs of electronics breaking into hotel rooms with the aid of assistant managers.

Blake had told his friends that if Boy Bush got elected he'd flee America. They'd laughed, assuming the prospect of Bush's ascent unlikely at best. After the debacle in Florida, after the Supreme Court's coup and Gore's meek withdrawal, Blake had contacted a former history prof, a Cold Warrior whose politics Blake abhorred but whose fundamental decency and principled nature Blake had always admired. Dr. Procházka, a Czech émigré from the Prague Spring, had taught for more than thirty years at the University of Michigan where Blake had earned his English Lit B.A. in the mid-nineties. Procházka, one of those exceedingly accessible profs who makes a point of hanging out with students, indeed, doing much of his best teaching over pitchers of beer, was forgiven his staunch conservatism, especially by his more sophisticated students who, for the most part, understood that, regarding Procházka's life, the distinction between "left" and "right" got heaved down an ideological rabbit hole that was Central European modern history, and that the Party, forming a kind of fire line, had done the heaving.

Procházka, delighted by the election results and recently returned from his latest visit to post-Velvet Revolution Prague, had been happy to assist his trust-funded former student in finding proper digs in Prague. Blake sublet Miroslav Procházka's ex-brother-in-law's flat in the Prague 6 Vinohradská district, and promptly struck up an affair with Procházka's niece, who had grown up in that flat. Suzanka, not quite so short that she qualified as a "little person," could press her forehead into Blake's sternum standing straight, though her body was *Playboy* voluptuous, that of a Marilyn Monroe circa 1953, in miniature.

"Hey, what do you do when a blind gypsy stands next to you waiting for the light to change?"

The jokester, a Czech exchange student named Igor who incessantly half whispered asides in Czech to his elder countryman, had beamed as he awaited his cue for the punch line.

"I think I know this one," Procházka had smiled.

Clap! Clap! Clap! Clap! Clap! had been the punch line. Bemused stares. Procházka had groaned and grinned, then explained that in Prague a clapping or clicking sound accompanies the green walk signal. By clapping, someone standing near the blind gypsy could compel the fellow to walk into traffic.

No joke, explained, is funny, and the racist underpinning of that particular joke had been lost on no one.

"If someone told such a joke here in the States," lovely, blond, and sincere-to-a-fault Brandy commented, "about an African-American blind person . . ."

"We don't have those clicking things at crosswalks," Landon, dumb as wheat germ yet a savant regarding the particulars of nineteenth-ccentury southern American history, had chimed.

"That's really quite beside the point," Procházka had said, and was correct. "It is no less racist, and yet the context of Czech racism against Roma is radically different than that of racism against African-Americans in the United States."

Milton, the only person of color at that eight-top in the Sweet Pea Pub in Ann Arbor, mumbled, "My black ass."

"Explain the difference," Blake had insisted. Three pitchers had graced the round oak table. Two were empty, one half so. Procházka had gestured toward the bar for another pitcher.

"Simple. Africans were brought to the New World against their will and turned into slaves. The Roma who arrived in the Czech lands chose to come, and were never turned into slaves."

"Mirek," Blake had said, "you're not saying that *that* historical difference in any way justifies racism against Roma."

"It doesn't justify, but it does explain. Roma are interlopers. Theirs is a culture of thieving and subterfuge. When they choose to assimilate, truly assimilate, they will become Czech."

"So they're not now Czech? Those who were born in Bohemia or Moravia are not Czech citizens?" Blake had pressed.

"Of course they are citizens. But they are not Czech." Procházka had spoken as though his pronouncement were self-evident.

"So, is it the case that African-Americans are U.S. citizens, but not Americans? I mean, is any hyphenated American not, strictly speaking, American?"

Procházka had chuckled. "A classic apples/oranges comparison, my boy!" He had a handsome, big-featured big head. His hair was the color of dried hops.

Blake was being dismissed, and that was fine. Milton, disgusted, had flung three or four dollar bills on the table, swung into his pea coat and double-timed from the table.

Suzanka was naked, the sheet rumpled around her. Crispy Critter, Blake's seven-year-old calico he'd brought over from the States, lay splayed hilariously on its back above Suzanka's pillow. Blake rubbed his cat's fat furry belly. It stirred a bit, readjusted, rolled on its side toward the headboard.

"*Kdo je?*" Suzanka rasped, her eyes pressed into the pillow.

"Who do you think it is, Zizi?"

Blake had attended his friend's going home party alone because it had been Suzanka's, "Zizi's," turn to spend the night with and tend to her great-grandmother, her father's mother's mother. She and her three older siblings, as well as their father and two aunts, took turns spending the night with the ancient woman, whose days had been numbered for at least a decade. She'd been dying that long. It had become something of a macabre joke in the family: *Prababička* would outlive them all.

Blake sat heavily on the corner of the bed, Zizi's side. Her small, perfect ass was at his elbow. "I saw a man get beaten half to death."

Zizi stirred, turned slowly, stared at him.

"A little while ago. I was coming up the hill from the river. Just got off the Seventeen. An enormous Roma was walking ahead of me. He walked fast, especially for someone so huge. I saw him throw something into a hedge, then a black car rolled up and two Elvis impersonators jumped out and whupped his ass."

"Did they see you?" At first it seemed an odd question, but of course it was a good one.

I don't know how they could have missed me; I was only half a block away."

"You're lucky."

"Yeah, I guess I am."

"You're lucky the guy they beat up was gypsy." She pulled him to her, undid his jeans.

They had brunch at the Old Globe: eggs Benedict, rich coffee, mimosas with fresh-squeezed. They read newspapers, Zizi *Lidové noviny*, Blake *The Herald Tribune*.

"Did you mean that because the fat guy was gypsy the guys who jacked him up assumed I wouldn't say anything to the police?"

"Ano."

"You really believe that?"

"Yeah."

"So, if he hadn't been Roma, they might have kicked my ass?"

"Maybe."

"Maybe my ass."

"Maybe your sweet American ass is a bit too self-righteous and much too naïve." Suzanka was a tiny person with a huge presence. She wore whole rooms in the same spirit that some people wear loud sweaters. Zizi owned the spaces she occupied, deigned to share them with Blake. She rose to her feet to kiss him passionately as he remained seated on the wooden bench at the rear of the restaurant section of the bookstore. "Stay out of trouble," she said, ruffling his hair. She shouldered her huge lime-green purse and was off to spend the afternoon with her family at her mother's sister's *chata*. Most of her family spoke some English, but Blake accompanied Zizi only occasionally to family gatherings precisely because he could tell what a strain it was for everyone to switch to English. The family's time at the *chata* was for R & R, and Blake was sensitive to the fact that his presence caused at least a small degree of anxiety.

The son of a retired vice admiral, and the grandson of the inventor of an essential oil rig lubricant who became a senator of a sparsely populated western state, Blake had grown up on navy bases: Rhoda, Spain; Long Beach, California; Sasebo, Japan. His grandfather William's political career had long been over when Blake entered adolescence in Long Beach. A charter member of the John Birch Society, Grandpa Bill saw communists under every bed and manhole cover.

"Civil Rights Movement was rife with commies." It was 1985. Blake would soon turn sixteen. Grandpa Bill wore a burgundy polyester leisure suit and smoked a Cuban. His comb-over was dyed a hideous, unnatural black, and his bulbous nose spewed smoke dragon-like.

"What's a commie?" Blake was fucking with him. He was high and in no mood for Bill's diatribes.

"You know what a commie is, boy."

"Are the Iranians commies?" Blake was reading Marcuse's *Eros and Civilization*. He wasn't understanding much, but something about it made him think of *Dr. Zhivago*, the movie.

"You bet."

"But the commies don't believe in God, and the Iranians are all about Allah." His buddy Bert had had a gram of Lebanese hash. He was buzzed and famished. When Grandpa Bill died, Blake would inherit a fortune, would never have to work. Even though he was only fifteen, this circumstance seemed one not to trifle with, stoned or not, but he couldn't help himself. His grandfather was such a dick.

"Both are totalitarian. Both are theocracies. In the Soviet Union, commies worship the state; in Iran, the state worships a false god." Self-satisfied, former Senator William Koch blew a ring within a ring within a ring.

Blake had calculated that something was wrong with his grandfather's equation. How can "commies" equal "state" when the former worships the latter? He was stoned, but not that stoned. "Oh, now I understand, Papa." He'd never have to work for the rest of his life.

Monday afternoon, slave to curiosity, Blake parted the thick foliage as though it were a curtain. He did this again and again, working down the hedge.

He looked both ways, twice, thrice, pulled then the dark-green duffel from the tangle of thorny switches. Furtively, he made his way a block south to *Pancrác*, jumped on the 192 bus.

He began the four-story climb to his apartment. There was a communist-era lift that worked fine, but that scared the hell out of Blake, who was slightly claustrophobic and generally fearful of even the most state-of-the-art elevators. He, his mother and two sisters had gotten stuck on one for about forty minutes when he was five or six.

It was now dusk, the season transitioning between late summer and early autumn. The sepia sunlight through the art deco windows he passed at each floor matched his mood. He'd seen a man beaten mercilessly the previous morning, and he couldn't muster any grief. If he'd seen a little girl beaten, or a little boy, a little boy or girl in a wheelchair, say, would he feel horrified? Why was a fat, ugly man unlovable? Why couldn't he grieve that human being's violent treatment?

He poured three fingers of Slivovice, lay the bag on the unmade bed. Zizi wasn't, generally, a slob, but having grown up in that apartment she seemed more cavalier about its daily upkeep than she might otherwise be, though Blake couldn't be certain. He'd never been to her apartment, which she shared with her oldest sister and her oldest sister's "best friend," a lesbian lover everyone pretended was not.

Eight thousand euros and a notebook containing a tiny, tidy, cramped ledger kept partially in Cyrillic, partially in Roman alphabet but in a language—neither Germanic nor Latinate—Blake did not recognize. Hungarian? Finnish?

And stacks of hideous kiddy porn. It was redundant, like hell. The children, male and female, were dark. Their terror was frozen in the still photos. Blake couldn't look beyond the moment he became fully cognizant of the theme of the photos. There were several tapes among the photos. He didn't doubt what they contained.

Crispy Critter curled up in the plastic clothes hamper. She shed onto everything, and Blake's buddy Markey, craziest bastard he'd ever known, was so allergic to cats in general, and to Crispy Critter in particular, that he had to wear a surgical mask when he visited. He'd lift the mask with his index finger to toke off of Blake's one-hitter.

Blake sat on the toilet, pants around his ankles, contemplating his options. Crispy Critter stretched, lifted her head to gaze at him, and then closed her eyes again.

He'd spent his childhood protecting his body from his grandfather's lecherous gaze. Once, when he was three or four, his "papa" had bathed him. Blake had never been able to recall the actual event, but always recalled, quite vividly, its aftermath. He had howled and screamed with such passion that his nannie had rushed into the bathroom and, wrapping him in a towel, whisked him away, pressed like a beloved mummy to her breasts.

Papa never again bathed him, and Blake had remained, all his life, pathologically modest in the old man's presence. He would not "hit the showers" after handball with his papa; he would not "take a steam" with him on family vacations. No one, neither his father nor his mother nor his nannie, Bonita, who became simply the house manager as Blake entered puberty, commented on Blake's obvious discomfort around his grandfather in situations when Blake was not completely clothed, even when he wore trunks to a beach or pool. He felt the old man's gaze; he felt something extraterrestrial.

When Blake was nine or ten, he'd seen a TV movie about a couple who said space aliens had abducted them. They spoke of being probed, violated.

When Blake reached puberty, he no longer felt that his papa was a space alien. He no longer felt threat. The geezer turned into a grotesque clown, someone whose death would be Blake's liberation from all fiscal cares.

Markey had described being diddled by his Little League coach. "Yeah, the motherfucker told me my pecker was dirty, and that he needed to show me how to clean it. He said that if I didn't learn to clean it properly, it would get diseased and fall off. He said I had to be careful not to get pecker rot." He'd passed Blake the bong.

"You circumcised?"

"What the fuck do you think?" Markey Libowitz had responded, coughing smoke.

"Is every Libowitz a Jew?"

"No, there are fourteen who aren't, and they all live outside of Dallas, Texas, in a fucking Buddhist commune."

Markey's parents died in an avalanche skiing the Italian Alps in the early '80s. He was raised through puberty by a beloved maternal aunt, and could live modestly off of the insurance money well into middle age. He wrote poetry and had no ambition beyond having fun. He cheerfully admitted to a death wish. In three days he would return to Long Island, New York, to his aunt's palatial home. He would finish his third book which would be published by Holy Cow! Press out of Minnesota, and rekindle his relationship with the "love of (his) life," a second cousin with whom he'd been physically intimate since they were thirteen.

Blake would miss the crazy bastard. In his mid-thirties, Markey would not live to see fifty, Blake was fairly certain, unless his Jewishness kicked in. Unless he connected to that collective, atavistic will to survive, he would perish.

"The cocksucker had an eating disorder," Markey had asserted with a professorial air, brandishing a nearly empty liter vodka bottle at Kafka's grave in the New Jewish Cemetery. All the months they'd lived in Prague, and this had been their first visit.

"Yeah, he was skinny," Blake had remarked.

"No, I don't mean he didn't eat. He chewed until whatever he was eating turned to liquid. The guy had megadaddy issues."

Blake had known better than to press Markey, especially when his buddy was drunk, regarding the connection between obsessive chewing and oppressive patriarchs.

"The teeth mother naked at last," Markey had whispered; he often quoted the Minnesota poet Robert Bly inexplicably.

Tuesday morning, Blake pulled up his pants, washed his hands, and checked his face in the mirror. He shaved, brushed, and changed his shirt.

He didn't need the money. He left it in the bag. The police station was two and a half blocks away.

Reinhard Heydrich, Deputy Reichsprotektor of Bohemia and Moravia, famously dubbed the Czechs "laughing beasts," yet Blake had always marveled at how undemonstrative Czechs are in public, indeed, how dour. "Light laughter on the face, heavy sorrow in the heart," goes the old saw, though, it is said, Czechs reverse it. And yet every Czech man past forty walks the world as though an angel cups his testicles firmly in its bright shiny hand, keeping him on the verge of pain but not quite causing pain, just discomforting anticipation.

When the Angel of History has you by the balls, laughter is not recommended. But the women are also dour, Blake had observed, and as he shuffled west, toward the Holiday Inn and the Palace of Culture, from which the station was but a block north, Blake fixed upon a tall young woman; he was 6'2", and she was surely as tall as he, taller in heels. She wore a red skirt that cut high on her exquisite thighs, and her breasts were perfect. Her hair was dirty blond and luxurious; she seemed, from her profile, not to wear makeup, but she truly was a woman who needn't. She was a goddess, pushing a black pram, wearing four-inch heels.

How could she be so svelte so soon after giving birth? Blake fell back, crossed the street to be behind her. He crept closer, saw the child, perhaps eight months, sitting up under the hood of the pram, gumming a *rohlík*, a Czech roll that, a day or two old, was good for teething. Blake had seen legions of Czech babies and toddlers gnawing the nutritionless staple.

She paused before a plateglass window. He didn't want to be thought a stalker, so strolled past the pram. She studied bolts of shiny fabric displayed in the window of an austere, communist-era store. He glimpsed a tattoo on the nape of her neck: a crucifix wrapped in barbed wire.

The Infant of Prague is dressed each month in a different outfit; all of them are gaudily ornate. In the cathedral where the Infant is tended to, in

Malá Strana, one may purchase in the gift shop rosaries and Infant spoons, Infant coins, Infant postcards, Infant pens, Infant posters, Infant calendars, Infant refrigerator magnets, tiny Infants in drawstring bags.

Blake wanted to know her, know such a young and gorgeous mother who dressed with overstated class and was marked at the nape of her neck by a crucifix wrapped in barbed wire. But she was on another planet admiring bolts of shiny fabric. Blake didn't even want to have sex with her, necessarily. He wanted to talk to her, which probably would be impossible. Pausing to gaze at a restaurant menu on a door, he waited until she'd passed, followed her for a block and a half, and then peeled off when she turned and looked him in the eyes.

The police station was a block and a half from Vyšehrad. As Blake approached the entrance, four cops climbed into a Škoda compact, and as he always did on such occasions Blake wondered why in the world four cops would cruise the anything-but-mean streets of Prague crammed into a Škoda.

As the cops rolled away, Blake wondered, too, how much money they earned each month, and what would happen to the cash, and the other evidence, if he entered and plopped the duffel bag on the counter. But that wasn't his concern. His karmic duty was to relinquish the bag.

"You were following me," she said matter-of-factly. Face on, the sunlight behind her, she was not a goddess, just a very pretty young woman. She had doubled back to confront him. "Why?"

"Why do men follow women?" Blake responded rather weakly.

"To do them harm?"

"God, no. You're really pretty, and I just wanted to look at you. Forgive me if I caused you any discomfort. Your English is very good."

"My mother was Irish. Long story."

She wore no ring. The baby cooed. She wiped its mouth with a cloth diaper strewn across its pudgy legs. "Your baby is lovely."

"My sister. Long story. So, look at me."

"I beg your pardon?"

"You said you wanted to look at me. So, look at me. Don't stalk me. Look at me." Her accent was neither Irish brogue nor Czech. It was some hybrid, but quite clear, lovely.

"I saw your tat and thought of the Infant of Prague. I don't know, the crucifix, the woman-pushing-a-baby thing. I don't get the barbed wire. I mean, I guess I've seen it before, but I've never gotten the iconography, what it's supposed to signify."

"Buy me an ice cream."

They strolled past the police station, through the arch entrance into Vyšehrad. The pram stuttered over the cobbles. The child quietly played with her feet.
The woman said not a word, and Blake, lugging the duffel bag, was speechless.

She told the vendor the brand of ice cream she desired; Blake paid. They
sat at a table shielded by a large, dark-green umbrella. The baby fussed a bit,
but then went quiet.

"Your name?" Blake asked.

"She Who Loves Ice Cream."

"May I call you Cream for short?"

"She Who. Yes, I am Shewho."

"Okay. I'm Blake. But you may also call me He Who Doesn't Suffer
Horseshit." She was pretty, stunning, incredibly intriguing, but not worth
such silliness. No one was. "I have a gorgeous lover. I don't love her, but I like
her a lot and we don't lie to one another. I'm not sure I even want to have sex
with you, Shewho, but I'm a sucker for intrigue." She silently finished her nut
and chocolate-encrusted ice cream, then sucked the wooden stick, wrapped
the paper around it, tossed it in a can five meters away.

"Nice shot," Blake commented.

"What's in the bag? Returning from a trip?" She pulled a cigarette from
her blouse, a lighter as if from the air.

"Eight thousand euros and a lot of kiddy porn."

She looked puzzled as she dragged on her cigarette.

"Child pornography. There are photographs of adult males raping boys
and girls. The kids are Roma, I think."

Shewho stared off, puffed luxuriously, gave a Slavic shrug, similar to a
Gallic one though less histrionic, more truly a gesture of cosmic resignation.
"When I came back to give you shit for stalking me, you were staring at the
police station. Why?" She dragged and blew the smoke out the corner of her
mouth.

"I find it incredible that Baby Jesus brings toys at Christmas," Blake
answered. "I mean, a fat man in a red suit one can at least visualize. How do
Czech kids, how did *you* visualize an infant bringing toys?" He was serious. A
siren screeched, then quickly petered out. "Did you imagine the baby naked?
Did it float into the darkened room? Did it carry the toys in a bag? Did the
infant drag the bag through a window, down a chimney? I just want to know
how Czech children visualize the baby Jesus bringing presents on Christmas
Eve."

"My father was an atheist, like most Czechs. My mother was a former nun from Belfast. Long story." She crushed the cigarette into the wooden table. "I'll raise this little one. My sister. Long story." She rose, smoothed her clothes, touched her temples, and smiled vaguely. "I didn't have to see the mechanics of the baby Jesus bringing toys. He didn't bring me toys."

"What did he bring you? What did baby Jesus bring you?"

The chatter of a transistor radio that the ice-cream vendor hunched over distracted Shewho. She stared at the vendor's back. A profound sadness cascaded over Shewho's beautiful face. Alarmed, Blake breathed, "What is it?" The baby cooed, then wailed. Shewho rose, reached into the pram, lifted the child, and stood bouncing it lightly. She stared toward the statue of Libuše. The baby calmed.

"Baby Jesus brought me my father's sorrow, my mother's weakness."

"Has something happened?" The vendor phoned someone, spoke hurriedly; her voice was gilded with fear.

She who cradled the baby with one forearm, rummaged through a large paisley bag with the other hand. She extracted a bottle, sat again, and plugged the baby's mouth with the nipple. "My baby sister brings me my father's sorrow, my father's weakness."

A clutch of passersby gathered at the window, where the vendor spoke rapidly and nervously on the phone, intent upon the chatter from the transistor radio.

"What's happened?" Blake asked again

"Please let me have the bag," Shewho answered, gazing off.

An old woman, her spine ravished by osteoporosis, dropped her ice cream, clutched her withered face, and muttered, her eyes full of woe.

"What happened?"

"Give me your bag. I know what to do with it."

"Do you need the money?"

"Of course I need the money." The baby farted; her hair was jet black.

"Something's happened." The vendor switched off the radio and pulled down the screen, closing her little business. She was headed toward greater knowledge of whatever the radio had reported. "Tell me what's happened."

"It's not clear. Planes crashed into buildings in New York." She returned the baby to its pram. Stared off. Lit another cigarette.

"Planes?"

"Two commercial airliners."

It was a clear mid-afternoon. Puffs skidded across the blue. "What buildings?"

"I can use the money, and I know what to do with the other stuff."

"What can be done with the other stuff? It's evil."

"Baby Jesus will know what to do with it."

He positioned the duffel such that it nestled between the pram's hood and its handle. Shewho had to hold the handle to keep the pram from tipping backwards. As she pushed her baby sister toward four p.m., the conflagrations Blake that moment could not imagine torched the loins of vengeance.

"May I walk you home?"

She nodded, so they sauntered; Blake stuffed his hands in his jean pockets; Shewho pushed the black pram.

"How is the little one your sister?" The air of Vyšehrad seemed agitated, but that, Blake knew, was mere projection. Shewho didn't answer. The black-haired baby slept.

"Don't you think that's a fair question? I just gave you eight thousand euros. Doesn't that buy a few answers?"

"My mother was raped. She gave birth to this child. Now she's gone, and I'm raising this precious abomination alone, but with a little help."

"She's dead?"

"I don't know."

"How can you not know?"

"I've no idea what happened to her after she left."

"You have no idea where she went?"

"I have ideas. I just don't know for certain where she is."

"Do you think she'll ever return?"

"Not if she's dead."

"And if she's not?"

"Then she should be ashamed for having left us, ashamed enough never to return."

Two boys in the shade of an aspen (or what seemed to Blake an aspen) tortured a hedgehog with a magnifying glass. A narrow shaft of sunlight pierced the shadow of the shimmering leaves, focused through the lens and scorched the bristling fur. Blake pointed with his chin, "That's how serial killers begin."

"They won't become serial killers. They're Czech. They'll become accountants."

Her apartment building was a quarter mile away. She unlocked the door, and pushed the pram across the threshold; Blake followed, and when they arrived at the stairs, Blake lifted the front of the pram as Shewho deftly, in high heels, climbed the stairs backwards. Her flat was on the third floor.

Blake followed into the flat, trying not to breathe too hard, trying not to seem as out of shape as he was. Shewho pushed the pram into the bedroom, closed the door. "Tea?" she offered.

She put on something classical, Blake thought Brahms, though he wasn't certain. It didn't matter. Something dark and momentous had occurred that hour and he wanted Shewho to click on her TV. She placed a tray before him on the coffee table, poured tea from a porcelain pot into matching white porcelain cups.

"Who takes care of the baby when you work?"

"Her grandmother."

"Your grandmother?"

"No, hers."

Blake tapped his fingers on the coffee table before lifting the cup to his lips. "Why are you fucking with me?"

She sipped, smiled, closed her eyes for two beats, then opened them wide. "It's a long story."

"Then just tell me a short one! Are you saying the mother of the man who raped your mother takes care of the baby when you're stripping until six in the morning?" Her costume, resplendent with shiny red and golden beads, was draped across a dining room chair; at the center of the table, a fishbowl was stuffed with crinkled bills: crowns, euros, dollars.

"It's the least she can do, wouldn't you say?"

Blake scanned for the remote, then rose, leaned forward and pressed the large button below the screen of the ancient television.

"It has to warm up," Shewho said, cocking an ear toward the bedroom. She popped up to look in on the baby.

The chatter of the Czech commentator was annoying; Blake turned down the sound, witnessed the passenger jets hit their targets several times.

How would Alfred E. Newman, as Markey referred to President George W. Bush, respond to this? Who did it? Why did they do it? How did they do it?

Why did he find the sight of the jets penetrating the buildings thrilling? Why did he find this moment exhilarating?

As Shewho reentered the living room, Blake took in the whole of her, desired her mightily.

"What are you looking at?" she smiled coquettishly.

"Inscrutable you."

"Are you randy for mystery?" She pulled a clunky old remote from the crack of her chair, turned up the sound.

"Not really. Especially when it's so fucking contrived."

She smiled at this. "The World Trade Center," she said. "Have you been there?"

"Yeah. Then it's probably Muslims. They tried to take it out once before, and those guys just keep trying."

"Are you scared?" She lit a cigarette, blew the smoke away from Blake.

"Yeah, but not about this. I'm scared that I watched a fat guy get beaten half to death and I feel nothing for him."

"What do you feel about the people who got killed today?"

"Generalized horror, disembodied empathy. In other words, not a fucking thing. But that has nothing to do with my humanity. My humanity is a murdered fat guy, because they surely finished him off. He was probably an evil prick. He probably got what was coming to him." Blake hadn't told her anything about witnessing the beating, that the fat guy was the source of his largess, and the source of the stacks of vile images accompanying the cash. She didn't require clarification; he offered none. She stared off, beyond the TV, the looped images of disaster, and blew smoke luxuriously.

"It's a long story?" she finally said.

"No, it's not even a story. It has no beginning and no end. Like *that*," he finished, pointing with his chin to the bedroom where the baby now wailed.

Happy Girl

2011

In addition to the obvious, the only thing Alena Pechová's American father gave her was U.S. citizenship. She hadn't even known that she possessed dual citizenship until she'd happened upon a U.S. passport, sporting the photo of an infant, while spring-cleaning Uncle Petr's summerhouse. It listed her birth date and first name. Confronting her mother, she'd learned that her father had not died of testicular cancer, and that indeed he was American. Her father had been born and raised in the American city of New Orleans, not in Slapy, thirty minutes outside of Prague. The passport had expired many years ago, but proved remarkably easy to renew at the embassy in Prague 1. Her American name was Alena Rheams.

Her mother had wanted to protect Alena from the unsavory truth of her origin. But she finally relented, one stormy evening in autumn, and told Alena the story of her conception. Síma Pechová met the American in a jazz club on *Národní divadlo*, a couple of blocks from Tesco, in the fall of 1991. It was a time when the city was filling with young Americans; they rode the muscular dollar through Prague's serpentine streets "like drunken cowboys," Síma recalled. Alena's father played trombone in the excellent quartet booked for that month. Síma Pechová was out with her girlfriends, trolling American expat hangouts.

They had an affair. He returned to Prague as Alena was born. Bob Rheams acquired for his Czech-American daughter a U.S. passport then left for good. Alena of course wanted to know why her father had even bothered to return for her birth, but Síma could not or would not say.

Though Síma made her living interpreting and translating from Czech into English, sometimes though rarely the other way, Alena had heard her speak English only curtly and on two or three public occasions. Alena's own English was halting; she was an average student but an avid reader. Síma, too, was a reader. So much of Alena's childhood had been in their quiet flat in Smíchov, Síma reading in her black rocking chair, Alena splayed on the old red paisley carpet, usually on her stomach, her chin in her hands, a book held open below her by the pillow upon which she rested her elbows.

Alena grew up hearing her mother curse most things American. Americans are arrogant. Americans are the world's bullies. Americans are hypocrites. Americans are fat. Alena had met only a few Americans, but had seen them in throngs near the tourist zones of Prague. She'd recently snuck off to see new American movies, but hadn't liked them much, or had found the process of reading subtitles annoying given that her humble grasp of English created a distracting dissonance between what she read and what she comprehended aurally.

An inordinate percentage of females in the Czech Republic are, by any standard, beautiful. Why this is so is a mystery. There seems not to be nearly as many beautiful females, in the aggregate, in Slovakia, Poland, Austria, Hungary, and certainly not in Germany, and surely the same gene pool feeds into all of Central Europe. Síma and Alena, often mistaken for sisters in public, were so beautiful that even other women stared at them. Alena had acquired while quite young her mother's unease at being gawked. Síma was self-conscious about her beauty, uncomfortable in her beautiful skin, and so was her daughter.

Alena took for granted her mother's inscrutable nature. She had traced, so many times as a little girl, with her pointing finger, the tiny red swan tattooed onto Síma's left shoulder, but had not inquired as to the occasion and reason for its existence in more than a decade. Her mother was a repository of secrets.

"Where do we go when we die?" Alena was five.

"It's a secret," Síma told her.

"So you know?"

"Perhaps."

Uncle Petr was no blood relation; he was Síma's best friend since childhood, which is to say before anyone, even he, knew he was homosexual. He was the man in Alena's life and she adored him.

Petr and his current friend Ogden, an Englishman whose Czech mother made sure he spoke Czech growing up, had a happy fire going in the pit. Ogden did not speak Czech particularly well, but he communicated well enough for campfire chatting. Síma brought a plate of sausages, cut to be cooked, from the little country cottage in the front of the property that was framed on the east and south by woods. Everyone skewered a wad of meat and held it over the flames. There was rye bread, wedged tomatoes, sliced cucumbers in vinegar, a crock jar of mustard and, of course, beer.

"So, Uncle Petr, when are you getting your puppy?" Alena asked. She'd been asking since she was five. Petr had been promising to get a Lab puppy for thirteen years.

"When America wins the World Cup." He turned the skewer deftly. Alena had dreamed of that puppy into adolescence. This was the first time Petr had put it out of reach.

Ogden chuckled, but of course didn't understand the context. "The Yanks are getting better, chum."

Síma poured everyone more beer from the porcelain pitcher she'd given Petr for his birthday fifteen years ago, when he had hair. "Yours is done, my seedling. The charred skin is full of carcinogens."

"Everything is a little bit poison, Mama. Let the girl eat a proper Czech sausage in proper Czech fashion." Petr had given up long ago trying to mediate seriously Síma's controlling of every aspect of Alena's life, but sometimes he would joke to let Alena know that he was on her side.

Alena smiled a little wickedly and twirled her sausage in the middle of the flame. Petr and Ogden simultaneously withdrew their skewers. Ogden dollopped mustard onto both their plates. Petr readied their skewers with more of the fatty meat.

Alena grew up spending weekends and holidays at Petr's country place, his *chata*. She'd planted and tended a garden there as long as she could remember. Those tomatoes they were eating were her tomatoes, and they were perfect. The cucumbers were hers.

In fact, the whole place would someday be hers. All her life Uncle Petr had reminded her that when he passed from the earth she would own everything, and he was a modestly wealthy man. He was restituted the apartment building in Smíchov where he and Síma had grown up and where Síma and Alena had lived all of Alena's life. And he owned the land and the two little log cabins that constituted his *chata*. Alena knew every square meter of that patch of land, every root of every tree. The tableau of her and Petr and her mother, sometimes a current "friend" though often not, roasting sausages in that fire pit ringed by the same smooth, gray stones all of Alena's life, was the essence of familial calm and happiness.

"Do people have *chatas* in England?" she asked Ogden.

"Only the very rich," Síma answered for him.

"Well, some regular folks have modest summerhomes," Ogden said, "though not usually on this much land. The Czechs are particularly fierce weekend relaxers."

"What about America?" Alena asked.

"Some folks have something called 'timeshares.' Petr used the English phrase; his English was poor, not even as strong as Alena's, "but there it is almost exclusively the wealthy who have second homes."

The yappy little dogs two lots away began to bark and Petr rolled his eyes. Usually, when they got started after sundown, they would not quit for an hour.

"If you had a proper big dog, Uncle Petr, we could arrange to have her eat them," Alena suggested.

Dogs don't eat dogs," Petr rejoined stonefaced.

"But they do!" she exclaimed, then switched to English. "The Americans have a saying, 'It's a dog eat dog world.'" It took Petr a moment to comprehend.

"Do the British have that saying?" Petr asked Ogden.

"I suppose one hears it, but we could have imported it from the Yanks, for all I know."

Alena was getting a little tipsy from the beer. She'd fetched it two hours ago from the pub a half kilometer from the main road that ran the length of the river. It had been her job to fetch beer since she was physically able to transport full pitchers. She poured half a glass more; it was still chilled, effervescent. Síma was on the porch of the front cabin, talking on her cell. It was probably a lover, Alena judged from how her mother moved as she spoke; she was almost dancing. She always seemed to dance when she spoke to a lover on the fixed line at home or on her cell. Alena rarely heard her mother's end of such a conversation, and hadn't met any of Síma's lovers in years. When she was young, occasionally a man would stay the night, but as Alena entered adolescence Síma stopped bringing men home.

Czech identity is grounded in irony, though it being so was not an original intention. The hegemony of the German language, and German culture, in the Czech lands, was as an overbearing husband and father who did not at all understand the nature and effects of his power over a woman and children, could not imagine, even, another paradigm of familial power. The Czech national movement, like all national movements, was propelled by fathers, stern, paternal, more or less enlightened nineteenth century men like Josef Dobrovský and Josef Jungmann who centered identity upon a language, a Slavic dialect that thrived primarily due to the tenacity of rural grandmothers, *their* grandmothers and thousands like them, practical, physically strong women who ruled hearths. Through the nineteenth century into the twentieth, all significant, urban business got conducted in German, but cows got milked, chickens got killed and plucked, in a Slavic dialect so resplendent with diminutives that Poles to this day call it baby Polish.

"Did you meet my father, Uncle?" Funny she'd never thought to ask. He'd played along for years with Síma's fiction of a dead Czech father.

"Briefly."

"Is he handsome?"

"Quite."

"Did you hear him play?"

"No, Noodles. I saw him on the street with Síma once. That's all. I think it was in front of the Slavia. He was tall, very good-looking. A little Italian looking, something Mediterranean, anyway. He wore a blood-red shirt and jeans. And a wedding band."

This was new information. "Are you sure it was a wedding ring?" Alena was a little startled.

"Yes, lovebug. The fact that he wore it either speaks well for him or not, depending upon how you look at the situation."

"Mama dated him knowing he was married?"

At this Petr laughed, snorting. "Sweet, your mama *prefers* married men."

"Why?"

"Ask her yourself." Síma arrived, smiling, her love dance finished.

"Mama, Uncle Petr says you prefer married men. Is that true?"

"Yes," Síma answered, not missing a beat.

"Why?"

"Because they have someplace to go."

The Party controlled the cities, but it could not control the personal lives of Czechs who fled the cities on weekends and holidays for their *chatas*. In the country, even twenty minutes outside of Prague, one could relax, feel rapturously hidden from Big Brother. One could eat and drink. One could have sex. Unfettered by religious mores, being demonstrably the least religious population, large or small, on the planet, Czechs responded to the Soviet invasion and the subsequent period, hideously dubbed "Normalization," by having more sex, much of it, most of it, outside the bonds of marriage, especially if one were married. They had always been notoriously promiscuous, but following the squelching of the Prague Spring a kind of libidinal frenzy compensated for civic oppression. The intrigue of affairs was a kind of narcotic.

Síma had seen this in her own parents, even her grandparents. After her parents' divorce when she was eight, an unraveling that followed a series of half-heartedly hidden affairs indulged in by both progenitors, there marched a parade of her father's women and mother's men that continued into the present. The only survivor of her grandparents was her paternal grandmother, a petulant woman who had buried three husbands in addition to Síma's grandfather, a man who had achieved considerable rank within the StB, the Czechoslovak secret police.

In fact, both sides of her family had been high-ranking Party functionaries (a penchant for sexual intrigue had been a common feature of the lives of Party members and dissidents alike, as well as everyone occupying the "gray area," as the Czechs called it, in between): her mother and her father, all four grandparents. In college in the late '80s, she, indeed, had been an enthusiastic, highly active member of the Communist Party. In the fall of 1989, the world turned upside down. Her path to a shining career got decimated.

As kids, she and Petr argued politics with the passion of beloved, hard-headed siblings. The communists had taken away the building from his family, who were permitted to occupy a modest flat in a building that his paternal grandfather had ordered erected with hard-earned resources. Síma's rejoinder was the routine Party pap regarding exploitive landlords, the good of the many, etc. That they were always able to compartmentalize politics and everyday life ensured a lifelong friendship.

"My father didn't really leave without a trace, did he, Mama?" Her head was spinning a little, but not unpleasantly.

"You know this is not a subject I wish to discuss with you, my seedling, and certainly not in the presence of Uncle Petr's new friend," Síma answered, knowing that indeed having witnesses was precisely why her daughter felt emboldened.

"It's a perfectly legitimate question, old girl," Petr said, leaned his back against Ogden's knees. Ogden kneaded his neck and shoulders.

Síma never grew angry when pressed, but she never gave in, either. There was information she kept under lock in her heart and she clearly had thrown the key off the Charles Bridge years ago. Indeed, her equanimity could be infuriating, though it simply made Alena sad.

"You lied to me for years. I've known for less than a month that my father is not dead, or at least likely is not, and that he's an American who actually returned to Prague for my birth and to claim me as a U.S. citizen. I turn eighteen in nine days. If you will not tell me what I want to know, I will go to New Orleans and find my father. I will find the truth." Alena could scarcely believe that the words had issued from her own mouth.

A Google search had dredged some information, mostly mentions on club websites advertising performances. There were pictures of this or that band, but without their instruments, so Alena had tried to find the one she most looked like. She remembered a tall, swarthy, handsome fellow who probably was he, given that the others were black or short and bald.

Síma took a moment to process. "You don't have the money to make such a trip," she said.

"Sure she does!" Petr exclaimed.

Alena's heart quickened. Síma's lips grew thin.

"You would give her the money to travel to an American city filled with doped-up blacks who carry pistols?"

"Filled?" Petr sighed.

"That's a bit of a stereotype, Síma," Ogden wrinkled his brow.

"And more than a little racist," Petr finished. "But, yes, I will give her the money, darling."

"Well, it would be for nothing. He died several years ago. In Houston."

"You're lying, Mama! I've seen him!" Well, she *thought* she'd seen him. She hoped.

"What do you mean you've seen him?"

"On the Internet. I've seen his picture."

Petr's face turned quizzical. Alena had just queried him about her father's appearance. "Your description of him makes me certain," Alena answered his puzzlement. "I even have his email address," she added.

"Nothing good will come of your contacting that man," Síma sighed. "He'll only break your heart."

"Did he break yours, Mommy?"

"Your mother's heart is made of titanium!" Petr joked, but an uneasy quiet followed his words.

"No, darling, he didn't break my heart. He wanted to take you from me."

The fire crackled. A light breeze rolled through the woods and the pit momentarily flared.

Alena was speechless. Was Síma telling the truth? Pressed, would she offer details?

"You can't say such a thing," she finally responded, "and just leave it at that."

Síma gathered soiled dishes, utensils, and with unnerving equanimity turned and walked to the front cottage.

"Oh, my God, what do you know about this, Uncle?"

Petr drew three deep breaths in succession. "He wanted to take you back. That's all I know. He held you hours after you were born—men were not allowed in the birthing chambers back then. He passed me in the hospital corridor as I waited my turn to see you, hold you. He didn't recognize me from our brief encounter on the street, but I certainly recognized him. He had tears in his eyes."

"Why is Mommy such an asshole?"

"Síma is fiercely loyal and stronger than any man or woman I've ever known. She loves you fiercely, like a lioness. She is simply a little bit amoral."

"How can someone be a little bit amoral? One is either moral or amoral," Ogden said.

"You say this because you did not live here before 1989," Petr replied. "I'm no philosopher, but I fancy there is a difference between immorality and amorality. The first is a path to evil, the second has simply to do with believing that the end justifies the means. Or something like that."

Síma was on the phone again. Silhouetted by bulb light, again she performed her little love dance, this time in the window of the *chata*.

Carmen rolled up on her bike as stars filled the deepening dark; Alena could barely make her out, though she could hear Zima, Carmen's seven-year-old jet-black toy poodle, whimpering with joy. Carmen's parents' *chata* was a couple kilometers south, on the river. She and Zima would spend the night with Alena, as they often did. Síma and "the boys," as Petr and whatever man he was with were referred to by Alena and Síma, would sleep in the front cabin, Carmen, Zima, and Alena in the rear. This had been the arrangement since the girls were eight.

"Hello, Car!" Síma yelled from the cabin; she was now playing cards with the boys, a game Alena had no interest in, a game for which losing hands compelled the losers to knock back shots of Slivovice; a farting polka issued from an ancient transistor radio, and there was much frivolity wafting from the front cabin.

The embers in the fire ring throbbed as breezes slid across them. Alena lay on her side, transfixed by the glow. Zima scurried at her feet, then to her face, licking her cheeks and nose.

"Hello, cunt," Carmen greeted.

"Hello, cow."

Carmen lay down on the grass, spooned Alena. "I think I'm pregnant," Carmen whispered.

"You've never fucked."

"A boy," Carmen corrected.

"It's only fucking if a penis is involved."

"So boys can fuck girls, and boys can fuck boys, but girls can't fuck girls?"

"Precisely."

The little dogs two lots away started up. Zima, to her great credit, curled into Alena's belly rather than responding. "I hate those fucking dogs." Carmen held Alena tighter.

"No clouds," Carmen whispered.

"The stars fuck the darkness."

"So the stars are boys."

"Yes."

"So we're darkness."

"Yes. But there are no boys."

"No stars."

They rose. A door opened two lots away, and the yelpers entered the yellow light. The door closed. Carmen grabbed her backpack and Zima followed them toward the rear cabin. Alena veered five meters from the door, pulled down her sweats, squatted, peed. Carmen opened the knotty pine door, flipped on the light.

As always, and most intensely for a day or two after a hard rain, the cabin smelled of mildew and mothballs. There were two narrow cots; the girls pushed them together, as they'd done for most of their lives. A poster of a young Karel Gott hung on the wall by the door as a kind of joke. Opposite Gott was a poster in which a cartoon soldier shook hands with a cartoon farmer; it was a propaganda poster from before '89, and was also a joke, at least to the girls if not to Síma. On the broad wall facing the window hung a framed black-and-white photo of a young Madonna, naked. The girls' ritual was to kiss their fingers and touch the photo upon entering the cabin.

There were eight candles scattered about; Alena lit them and switched off the light. Síma called immediately to remind Alena to blow out the candles before going to sleep.

"No, I think I'll forget and burn down the cabin with us in it," she sassed playfully. Zima curled at the foot of the beds, in the seam between them.

"Did you write him yet?" Carmen asked. Her name was actually Jitka, but she'd fancied being called Carmen for the past three years, since seeing the famous opera at the National Theatre with her grandmother.

"I've started a letter, but I've never written anything in English. It's very difficult. I'll finish it and send the email when we get back to Prague. Mama knows I've found him, that I'm writing him."

"I can't believe Síma lied to you for so long." Carmen stepped out of her panties and Alena gasped and giggled. Carmen had shaved. "Everyone's doing it now. Didn't you know that? *Bush*," she said in English, "is so '90s," she finished in Czech.

"I'll keep mine, thank you. I've heard that shaving just makes it come back thicker." She stepped out of her panties, climbed under the sheet.

"Good day, Mr. Vaculík," Alena chimed. The old, famous dissident looked up from the dirt he was tending with a rusted spade; he was shirtless and gross, intent upon his gardening. He smiled and waved at the beautiful girl he'd watched grow up from a distance but whose name he could never recall. He waved again then continued turning the dirt.

He wrote feuilletons, little ironic essays that had appeared in samizdat, the underground literary network, before '89, but his writing now appeared in *Lidové noviny*. What he now wrote was grumpy and small, Alena judged. She hadn't read his samizdat writing, though Petr said that that work was edgy, funny, relevant. Síma, of course, found the early work boring and what he was writing now just silly. He was old and ugly the way old people just are. He was a little sloppy fat, but somehow regal. Yes, he was like an old king, an old lion. A chain link fence surrounded his property. He had numerous fruit trees and his vegetable garden was twenty meters by twenty meters. All her life Alena had glimpsed that old lion working in his garden. All her life she'd known that he was famous, at one time a famous opponent of the old regime, a way of life Uncle Petr, and almost everyone else she'd known who was old enough to remember, loathed, but for which her mother was nostalgic.

She passed the pitcher to the somnolent bartender, plopped a hundred and twenty crowns, in ten-and twenty-crown coins, on the counter.

"That's one beautiful chick," she heard a male voice say in English. She ignored the voice.

"Good thing she can't understand you, asshole," another male voice answered in English.

"Hey, girl, can we buy beer for you?" someone asked in bad Czech.

The bartender, Květa, let the foam settle before pulling the lever again. He was an affable idiot who stared at Alena's breasts and was otherwise no trouble.

She turned. Three American boys in the rear booth. What were they doing in Dobřichovice? No Americans ever came here. They were dressed like Americans. They had American smiles.

"Why you are here?" she asked in English.

"We are here to visit my *babička*, my grandmother," the one who had spoken bad Czech answered.

"I know what mean *babička*," she responded, *Idiot* implicit in her tone.

"Your English is good," a redheaded, freckled but otherwise pleasant looking fellow said.

"You lie," Alena responded.

"We're from America," the little dark-skinned one said.

"You think I cannot see you are American?"

There was half a glass left over. Alena knocked it back. It was cold and excellent.

"A girl after my heart," the dark one laughed. What did he mean by this? Why did he laugh saying it?

"I am American," she boldly asserted, and didn't know why. She could never explain what she meant to these American fools. She grabbed the pitcher with both hands. The redhead leaped from the booth and opened the door for her.

"Thank you," she said in Czech. For that second she forgot the English expression, but then recalled it. "Thank you," she repeated in English."

"May I walk with you?" he asked.

He wanted to accompany her. He was asking permission. "Yes." Perhaps he would carry the pitcher.

"That looks heavy," he said as they turned onto the kilometer-long, twenty-degree incline back to Petr's *chata*. What is "heavy"? How can a pitcher "look"? "Allow me," he said, and carefully gripped the pitcher from the bottom. She let him take it. "So, you're American?"

"I am here all my life. My father is American."

"Cool. Where's he from?"

"New Orleans."

"Totally cool. I love New Orleans! I did Jazz Fest this past spring."

Jazz was the kind of music her father played. What is a fest? Cool is good, she knew. "My father is jazzman," she asserted with a pride she didn't quite understand. "I do not like boys," she blurted.

The redhead wrinkled his brow. "My name is Link," he said.

"My name is Alena. I like girls."

"Well, we have that in common," he said, and smiled bemusedly.

She didn't understand, though she found his smile funny, and smiled back.

"I'm glad it's not hot today," he said, but she didn't immediately understand his pronoun reference, but then did.

"It is good day," she responded, knowing that most summer days she'd be sweating at this point in the climb back to Petr's.

"Will you have someone to help you drink this *pivo*?" Of course this was the only Czech word an American boy would know.

"My mother and uncle will drink. My friend will drink. She is naked in sun."

"Tanning?"

"What do you say?"

"She is pretty with no clothes on?"

"She is beautiful always."

"What does your father play?" Children play, but she recalled that one plays a piano. She gestured sliding.

"A trombone! Very cool."

A hard breeze rustled the trees. A storm was rolling from the east. Alena smelled rain. "You must go," she said, halting. She reached for the pitcher. Link relinquished it, then dug into his back pocket, pulled out his wallet, plucked from it a card that he presented to Alena. She could not hold the pitcher with one hand, so set it on the road and took the card.

Link Browning, Esquire
Cool Dude
link.browning@gmail.com

"I'm an exchange student at the Anglo-American University." What was an esquire? She'd heard of Anglo-American University. It was respected. What was exchange?

"Thank you." She smiled formally and slipped the card in her pocket. Then she stooped to lift the pitcher.

"You are very beautiful," Link blurted.

"I know," she said, rose, and walked on. The clouds were pushing in, and the first small thunder rattled the air.

> *Sir:*
>
> *My English is not good, but I will try to say to you what I need to say. I think you are my father. I think I everything have seen of you on Internet and you are that man. If I am wrong please tell this to me and I bother you no more.*
>
> *I am good girl. I am not grate student but I love books. Somday I want to right a book but I don't knowhat about yet. Soon I will eighteen be, but not sure what to do after school. I am full of question marks!*
>
> *My mother Síma is good but maybe little amoral. You problemly know this if you made me with her.*
>
> *Mama said my father died from cancer when I was baby. I discovered you in recent times. I have a wonderfull uncle that is not my uncle but he love me like he is my uncle. He is Petr, and I much love him.*
>
> *When a little girl I want father very much. When little I want a father to read to me and hold my hand and walk with me in park. I guess I want you, but I did not know you, but may be some way I did. No matter how much love, uncle is no father.*
>
> *I can not belief you American! My mother not like Americans. She some time say terrible thing about America.*
>
> *I have courage to write this to you because my uncle told you wanted me. Did you want me? Just to know you want me when I was baby will make me happy girl in Czech Republic!*
> *Alena Rheamsová*

Alena couldn't send such a missive to her father. She knew it was full of errors, that she would embarrass herself. He would think she was an idiot. But Simá certainly wouldn't edit it for her, and she didn't know anyone else whom she trusted and whose English was good enough to help her make the letter good.

She printed it out and read it over several more times. She was able to make a few corrections. She changed "right" to "write," put in some articles, which is always tricky because Czech doesn't have any. She understood the difference between the definite and indefinite article, yet still found it difficult to know when to use which. And she understood that Czech being a highly inflected language does not require as heavy a reliance upon syntax as does English.

Alena wished profoundly that she had been more serious about studying

English, that she had read more English, especially. No, she could not send such a terrible email letter to her father.

She recalled Esquire. She raced to her room and pulled the jeans she'd been wearing at the *chata* from the floor of her closet. The card was in her front pocket.

> *Dear Link Browning, Esquire*
> *I need help on letter for my American father. I said to you I not like boys but it is difficult. Please come to Bohemia Bagel in Smíchov. Americans like it and is close to university. Please come 14:00 tomorrow.*
>
> *Alena, the girl you did meet in Dobřichovice.*

He hadn't written her back an email, as she'd thought he might. She arrived fifteen minutes early, purchased a cup of green tea. She brought the letter in an old school valise. She was nervous.

He arrived exactly on time. He was dressed nicely, for her: a black shirt and jeans, black shoes that shined. He had groomed: His ginger hair, medium length, shined, too.

"Ahoy," he said, reaching to shake her hand.

"Dobrý den," she answered, and inserted her hand limply into his.

"Gimme a second," he mumbled, raising his index finger. He strode to the counter and purchased a double espresso.

"You live around here?" he asked.

"I live close. With my mother. Where in American you live?" She was being polite. She didn't care. He seemed nice enough, but what she wanted from him was his English.

"I'm from San Diego. Do you know where that is?"

"It is south to Los Angeles." The Czech schools teach geography very well. "On Mexico."

"I'm impressed. Before I came over here, if you'd asked me where Olomouc was, I'd have been clueless."

She wasn't quite certain what he was saying. "I don't understand, Link Browning, Esquire. Will you help me on my letter?"

"Not much for small talk, heh? He grinned and shook his head. "Let's see it."

She pulled it from the valise, handed it to him. As he read, his brow furrowed.

He took a deep breath. Stared off. "No," he finally said.

"No? I will pay you!" she blurted.

"Your letter is beautiful. I'd only fuck it up if I edited it. It's authentic. The emotion is real and honest."

Alena's eyes watered. "You will not help me."

"You don't need help, is what I'm telling you. If I edit your letter, what will you do when he writes back?"

Funny that she had not considered this simple, extremely important point. "My father will think I am stupid."

"You're wrong! You told me the guy's a jazzman. Plays slide trombone. He's from New Orleans, for chrissake! That letter of yours is going to sound like a beautiful solo."

"You are crazy," she said. She'd never seen such red hair. His eyes were light blue, expressive. She wasn't certain what he meant, but he seemed sincere. "What do you study?" She was genuinely curious.

He smiled hugely. "Literature."

"You read poetry and novels?"

"Something like that."

"Do you want to write books?"

"No. Well, yes, I want to read books then write about them. So, you're not attracted to guys?"

"It's difficult."

"Do you mean complicated?"

"Yes, I mean that word. Complicated."

"Will you go to a movie with me?

How many times had boys and men vied for her attention? How many times had males fawned over her? "What movie?"

He said the title of a recently released American movie that was showing with Czech subtitles. "Okay," she said. "But I will not do sex."

He seemed taken aback, flustered. "Of course not," he managed to stammer.

She told him she'd meet him at the Angel Mall theater complex at six o'clock tomorrow. She slipped the letter into the valise, rose, nodded to him, and exited the shop.

She walked down to Kampa. Stared into the Vltava. Ducks gathered, anticipating bits of bread. She would make a friendship with Link Browning,

Esquire. If he would not edit her letter, she would use him to improve her English. He was nice. She could tell that he had a good heart. Carmen would like him.

She was not unhappy. She loved Prague. She loved her mother, though couldn't wait to get away from her. She loved Uncle Petr. She loved Jitka, who was like an intimate sister. She loved the Vltava, its ducks and swans.

But there was a part of herself she did not know; it was a huge mass of information that was her birthright. It was powerful and sinister. It was open and sustaining. It was a source of books and movies and bad television shows that got dubbed into Czech. It was fast food and religious fervor. It waged wars and liberated. Too many of its people were fat. Too many knew nothing about the rest of the world. It stretched from ocean to ocean. It was a place of much laughter and hope. It sent people into space, to the moon. It was where girls were free but not safe. It was a place for starting over, being new.

She was Alena Pechová. She would craft an Alena Rheams. In her heart there was velvet darkness, and upon it there were stars.

Chunk

2012

The victim of a recurring nightmare, Don returned to Solana Beach after three years in the Czech Republic. One of only two committed surfers in that landlocked country of ten million, he had literally dreamed, those nights he'd not been visited by his nightmare, of ocean swells. He'd chased his high-school sweetheart there, gotten dumped, and remained, for the first months, in Prague apprenticed to the great Czech puppet maker and puppeteer Miroslav Trejtnar. For the next thirty months he'd smoked blunts, whittled, and spent roughly a third of his modest inheritance on living reasonably well in Prague.

Even as he'd drunk himself to death, Don's father had taught him the fundamentals of working with wood, and long before arriving in Prague Don had been a consummate whittler. Most of his adolescence, when not climbing then sliding down walls of water on a waxed fiberglass board, had been spent stoned, slicing curls from blocks of wood. He'd sold anatomically perfect effigies of horses, dolphins and naked women at swap meets, earned enough to stay stoned and not to starve as he'd awaited his father's death and his own subsequent inheritance.

After his father's passing and after having spent seven years in and out of Mesa Community College, Don had been relieved to drop the charade of student status. The ancestral home in pricey Solana Beach had been easy to lease for a decent monthly. Above the garage behind the house was the efficiency apartment he'd occupied through high school and almost a decade after. He'd written into the lease of the young family occupying his ancestral home his prerogative to occupy the efficiency unit.

That first morning after his arrival home, he awoke from his nightmare and from jetlagged stupor, shivered slightly with excitement as he pulled on his wetsuit; he'd put on only a few pounds in Prague, but he could feel each one in the skintight black rubber. He waxed his board and strapped it to the rack of his '99 Volvo. Anticipating a dead battery, he'd enlisted a bro by email to charge it a couple of days ahead of his return. He picked up that friend, Scott, who, in his early thirties, lived with his widowed mother on the edge of the Solana Beach golf course. Don and Scott greeted one another with a quick, cool hug.

"Dude, you were gone too long."

"I just lost track of time, bro." Don strapped his buddy's board to the rack and they headed down the long hill toward I-5 South; Solana Beach's actual beach area was small; they'd do La Jolla.

The sun was low in the east as they hit the freeway, only forty minutes ahead of the darkness of predawn. It was mid-week, and the traffic was already busy, though an hour from being thick, two from packed lanes of self-interested, mean-spirited commuters.

"I'm sorry about Beth," Scott said, staring at the road through wrap-arounds. Don and Scott had never been particularly close, but Scott was easy to be with; he was a casual surfing bro, never a wingman, but a solid dude Don had known since junior high. Don plucked a joint from the pocket of his Hawaiian shirt—he'd vacuum packed a half ounce of good shit and stashed it in the wall of the efficiency three years ago—and lit it with the car lighter.

"Yeah, it was a fucking wipeout, but I got over it." That Scott even knew Beth had dumped him for the Czech drummer of a Munich-based heavy-metal band irked, but his knowing was only because Beth was a good friend to Scott's sister Lou. "I saw plenty of action in Bohemia, dude. I wasn't crushed for long."

And he had indeed seen plenty of action. He'd gotten laid a lot, and over the last nine months had settled in with a pretty, fiery Australian, Baily, who worked in Prague as an office manager of an alternative energy firm. Surfing, lamenting that they could not surf in Central Europe, had been their primary bond beyond sex.

The swells were modest, which Don assumed, as he traversed the beach, was probably a good thing given his hiatus. But once out, once he'd caught a rare five-footer, three years of inactivity on the ocean evaporated. He was home. Everything was okay again. Everything would be okay.

His apprenticeship had been an enlightening disaster. His gift for shaping wood far surpassed that of anyone in Miroslav Trejtnar's workshop, including the master, and yet it was under the master's truncated tutelage that he'd learned that though he, Don Cook, was a gifted, obsessive, intuitive craftsman, he was not an artist.

He could not, as could the master and as could the master's star apprentices, craft effigies that transcended craft, which came alive as markers of human fallibility in all its glory.

That night, watching *Celebrity Apprentice,* Don shaped a six-by-six block of balsa into the Silver Surfer of Marvel Comics. He worked with a five-blade set of surgical scalpels he'd ordered online from an outfit called Micro-Mark. He usually worked with a *pfeil* Swiss-made Brienz Collection, twenty-five-piece, full-size carving tool set, though he'd been curious about surgical scalpels, and was learning that they were, as he'd expected, quite subtle, though as he worked he feared their fragility.

His gift for coaxing recognizable shapes from blocks of stuff had dazzled Beth when they were in high school. Once, during detention—she'd been there for mouthing off to an English teacher over a legitimate political point; he'd been there for sheer indolence—he'd whittled a unicorn from a cake of soap he'd filched from the faculty restroom. She'd sat awestruck as the bar of Ivory transformed, by virtue of a two-inch pocketknife attached to Don's key chain, into a perfect, miniature mythical creature. Finished, without a word, he'd reached across the aisle and stood it on the desk before her wonder-filled eyes. When the grumpy track coach/shop teacher who'd pulled after-school detention duty noted the mound of white shavings on Don's desk, a day's detention became a week's, but impressing that gorgeous, classy girl had been worth an entire semester of detentions.

Don's disengagement from apprenticeship had simply been the result of the fact that Trejtnar, after three months, had had nothing else to teach Don. Or, more precisely, there had been nothing else that Don had been intellectually or intuitively capable of learning. The mechanics of puppets/marionettes didn't interest Don beyond a certain point, and the idea of actual performance, stagecraft for effigies, he'd found distasteful.

When his mother asked to be his friend on Facebook, just days before his return to Solana Beach, he'd felt the old rage. In two minutes of screaming mayhem, he'd dismantled twenty marionettes in various stages of construction. The floor of his flat had resembled the scene of a car bombing. Two and a half years of subtle, excruciatingly detailed work had sprawled twisted, ripped and torn asunder over the grungy linoleum.

When she'd requested again the night before his departure, he'd drunk a liter of Slivovice and wept convulsively unto oblivion.

The next morning, an hour before his taxi was to arrive, she'd again requested to be his friend. He'd sent her a message: *How dare you.*

"Fucking Donald Trump," he whispered to the Silver Surfer and finished off the front curve of the board. Shavings filled the little trash can he'd whittled into since high school. Alfred E. Neuman's tranquil headshot was emblazoned on both sides of the oval. "Why does the motherfucker even bother with this shit?" He changed the channel to a Padres game, but felt disconnected; in Prague, he'd not kept up with the team's trades and drafts. It was a different team than the one he'd left.

Don wasn't particularly concerned that he didn't have the art gene, or whatever. He was proud of his skill, but not excessively, annoyingly so. Whittling was an obsession, he guessed, as far as he understood what an obsession was. It kept him centered, kept his highs focused and edgy. It was what he did between surfing and not surfing, *between* in the sense of a partition on one side of which lay despair, his nightmare, and on the other contentment.

His months in Prague had been purgatorial, as he understood purgatory to be a place of waiting, a kind of dentist's office strewn with dated magazines. Prague was a beautiful place, though he'd grown numb to that particular kind of beauty quite quickly. He'd followed Beth there despite everything, despite the betrayal, despite the fact that he'd often fantasized beating her senseless for that betrayal.

Beth had left Prague with her mother and father and two brothers when she was five; by 1988 the totalitarian regime had become rather clownish, though no one could have imagined it withering away in fewer than twelve months. A talented aeronautics engineer, Beth's father had immediately scored a job with Northrup, and the family had put down roots in the hardpan of San Diego.

Beth's return centered on her strong desire to reconnect with family, and to reawaken the language of her early childhood, and Don had marveled at her rapid progress from halting, awkward, slow Czech to something approaching fluidity in only a few months. Beth had majored in political science at University of California San Diego and had made the dean's list every semester, but had not begrudged Don the fact that he hated school. She was proud of his gift for carving, and had pushed him hard to work with Trejtnar.

"The guy's a genius, baby cakes," she'd insisted.

"I don't give a fuck about fucking puppets," had been his blunt reply.

"Don't you see that much of what you do is very similar to puppet making? The history of Puppet Theater in Bohemia is rich and deep. Can't you appreciate it?"

Of course that was not a question Don would even try to answer. But he would seek out Trejtnar, give the puppet thing a shot.

He tried mightily to put the horror behind him. Slowly, their lovemaking resumed. The distance did not aid healing so much as blur perspective. The Pacific Ocean called him, but it did so as though his heart were a telephone and the ocean were mindful of the cost.

Beth had left him because her presence in his life drove him down, held him pinned on his back in the sand. She'd known she was the big one, the killer, the last ride. She loved him too much to kill him. She'd left a note:

I regret nothing but your regret. What happened wasn't evil, just weird, and it was beautiful. The beauty is what torments you. I hope, darling, that someday you are reborn onto your incredible gift.

"So this swamp monkey from like Iowa or something hits on my main surfette Vicky and when she stuffs him he like gets all Bruce Willis trippy on her and I had to . . ."

Don hadn't chilled with his tribe for three years. Butchy was cranking out the bullshit like it was soft-serve Tastee-Freez, and it was cool because that was Butchy's job. He was an affable idiot and his bros loved him.

"That's tight, bro," Maurice said dismissively, but with affection. Butchy shut up long enough to hit the bong.

Maurice and Don had been tight. They'd been each other's wingman. Don's retreat had mystified Maurice, who'd simply given him space. The move to Prague Maurice had known was sick, but he was loyal and just backed off. They were trying to reconnect now. Maurice hit the bong and passed it to Benny, who hit it and passed it to Burney.

"Give me the lighter, motherfucker," Burney said to Maurice.

Everyone had assumed his position in Don's space. After taking a hit, Don resumed whittling. He'd always whittled when the tribe was together passing the bong. The dudes accepted that that's just the way it was going to be at Don's crib.

"Whatcha workin'?" Maurice asked, letting out just enough smoke to form the question.

"I'm trying to do something original," Don responded. Maurice was puzzled.

"Will I recognize it?"

"Good question," Don paused, the scalpel hovered about the balsa chunk. "If it's original, you shouldn't be able to recognize it the way you can probably recognize that new piece over there . . ."

"Yeah, dude, that's Silver Surfer!"

"Okay, well, it won't be something like that, but maybe you'll recognize it another way."

"Don't get spooky on me, Don Mon!"

"Fuck you, Maurice," Don grinned, and chipped away.

"Fuck you, too, son!"

Don had been encouraged to call his parents by their first names from the time he was a toddler. Early on, he'd been puzzled by his friends' puzzlement, but "Fabe" and "Matty," for whatever reasons, had been more comfortable having Don address them by their nicknames.

"Matty, what's for dinner?" Don would ask.

"Ask Fabe. It's his night to cook," she might answer. Don would go to his father's office, and Fabe would be passed out on the carpet, an empty fifth bottle above his head.

"Fabe's not cooking tonight," he'd matter-of-factly inform his mother, who'd be deep into *The Wall Street Journal*. A successful investor, Matty had wielded her MBA from USC with considerable skill.

"You want to grab a bite at that new fish place?" she'd inquire without looking up from the stock lists.

And so Matty and Don had eaten out a lot, became pals through Don's adolescence. His mother was a fetching middle-aged woman, and Don and Fabe had both been aware that she was sexually active and adventurous. They'd asked no questions. She'd told no lies.

"Some eggs?" An early riser, usually from his office floor, Fabian made good breakfasts for his son. Today being Sunday, Don had poured into the kitchen well past nine. Fabe had been sipping coffee, listening to *Meet the Press* turned down low on the small TV on the kitchen counter next to the toaster oven. Don had noticed that his parents' bed was made. Matty had been out all night.

"Where's Matty?"

"Eggs?" Fabe repeated. Sometimes, just for the sake of a little mischief, Don would note how fucked up his parents' marriage had gotten.

"Poach 'em, okay? Soft." He would spend six sober hours with his father, good, quality time in the garage before five p.m., before Happy Hour.

Matty moved out in the middle of Don's junior year. She bought a sweet bungalow, a two bedroom, two baths with vaulted ceilings, skylights, just seven blocks away. Don grew comfortable having dinners with his mother, watching movies, just hanging out. Well past high school, he and Beth spent easy time there with Matty and whomever she was attached to, sometimes men only a decade or so older than Don, sometimes women. Lovers flowed through Matty's life. She even stopped by the ancestral home from time to time to look in on Fabian, who was staggering gently into each perfect, southern California night.

As she attended UCSD, Beth had kept an apartment near campus; the brief commute to Solana Beach she'd make on most long weekends (she was able to manage Tuesday/Thursday schedules most semesters) that did not require her to hole up in the library. Her parents had moved to Cleveland soon after she'd graduated from high school, and during her college years made frequent trips to Prague. They'd talked of moving there more or less permanently.

Don had been fine with the arrangement. His own bogus college career, a sick concession to his sick father, limped from semester to semester. He'd whittled days, weeks, months, years, until the night Fabian ate a bottle of Ambien he chased with a fifth of Grey Goose that he did not, for once, finish. The legal matters took a while but concluded nicely. Don found perfect, long-term tenants. He surfed. He whittled. He loved his woman. He loved his mother. He loved his bros.

"Why would you go over there without me?" Don asked.

"Matty and I have a friendship independent of you," Beth replied.

"What does that mean?"

Beth's Focus had been parked in Matty's driveway at four in the morning. Returning from a party, Maurice had seen it and had assumed Don had been there, too; he'd mentioned seeing the car in a phone call earlier in the day.

"It means she's my friend," Beth said.

"Do you have to be friends with her behind my back?"

"Friendship requires some privacy."

"What the fuck does that mean?"

"It means Matty and I don't need, don't want our friendship filtered through you, our love for you."

In his recurring nightmare, Don is encased. He strains to move, but that which holds him is molded perfectly to the contours of his body and he is unable to extricate any part of himself even by a single centimeter. Then he remembers to open his eyes and he is on his back in the sand and waves are breaking far above him.

After surfing, and after trashing the "original" piece he'd begun the night before, Don drove directly to the storage unit that contained his father's stuff, what was left after the estate sale, and a few things that hadn't been for sale. The unit faced east, so Don did not require a flashlight to rummage. Sunlight bathed the stacks of plastic crates and tools, the boxes of books.

Fabian Cook had authored eight critically successful novels; two had been turned into blockbusters for which he'd helped to write the screenplays. *Gray Tide* had been the big one, the one that had allowed him to settle into Solana Beach and drink himself toward extinction.

At the rear of the locker, behind the detritus of a wasted life, squatted a four-foot tall, five-foot diameter chunk of lacquered oak, Fabian Cook's office end table. It had not been something precious to Don's father; it had stood in the corner of the room supporting an oval glass top; on the glass had been a photograph of Don's parents flanking his four-year-old self. His entire adolescence Don had coveted that chunk of wood, had imagined it containing a dolphin breaching a swell, or a Venus stepping gloriously naked from a giant shell on the surf's edge.

For the almost three years he'd spent in Prague, Don had fashioned perfect Giovannis, perfect Kafkas, perfect babičky, perfect witches, perfect devils, perfect Havels, perfect Klauses. Some he sold, most he gave away. In spring and summer, he would get stoned and take his materials and his tools to Kampa park, spread a blanket on the grass, and in the midst of lounging lovers and children playing, in the midst of dogs chasing balls and Frisbees, he worked. Often, children gathered, and following the children their parents, and as the audience came and went there seemed a general consensus of quiet appreciation, quiet reverence, even.

He made a messy path from the rear to the unit's opening, gingerly dragged the hard wood through that path and wrestled it into his trunk, tied the trunk with a cord he ripped from a piece of dated electronics.

Getting it up the steps to his space had been exhausting; he'd rested five to ten seconds on each of the fourteen steps. It had barely fit through the doorframe. Now it defined his small living space by its presence.

He laid out his tools, smoked a joint, and for the second time in his life began whittling and chiseling with absolutely no idea as to what would emerge from the wood.

Ghost in My Heart

2005

Marty needs to name his band; it has to be something that most hip Czechs will recognize. He is good at titles and band names, he's been told, and trusts his intuition to dredge something from his fecund unconscious. *Tender Gland* bobs to the surface. Three syllables. An adjective-noun combination. Appropriately lurid, but also medical, evocative of terrifying sickness and as such too easy to goof on, even or especially for Czechs. *Electric Languor.* Oxymoron. Pretentious, too literary. *The Mystic Pigs.* The Czechs love their pork. They'd laugh their asses off. *The Sons of Betty Crocker.* Too long, weird in a bad way. *Angel Meat.* This is the first name on his list of keepers. *Brown Susan.* Where did that come from? He doesn't even bother googling it. *Dirt Nap.* This is the second name on his list of keepers. *The Pecker Woods.* Wouldn't travel very well, especially back to the States. *Hair Pie.* Anachronism. Gone the way of the turntable. They all shave now. *Enemies of Leisure.* But the band would want to be just the opposite, and *Allies of Leisure.* . . . He writes it down on his list of possibles. *Ghost Monkeys.* Doesn't want that '60s pop culture association, though he likes the sound. *Ghost Heart* or *Ghost in My Heart.* The former seems contrived, but the latter is, he chuckles, haunting. It's weird in a good way. He googles it, and of course there are a couple of obscure song titles, but no band with that name.

"Ghost in My Heart," he announces to the band, "that's our name."

"Your heart?" says Rex, the drummer. His name is Petr, but he decided last week that everyone should call him Rex.

"Everybody's heart," Marty shoots back.

"I don't give a fuck," says Frank, the other American in the band. "We could call ourselves Marty and the Ass Wipes and it wouldn't matter." He lodges the filter of his half-smoked cig in the taut strings of his bridge and continues tuning.

Marty waits for the mumble of Rex translating the exchange for Mikel, the bass player, to finish. Mikel snorts a laugh as he responds. "What'd he say?"

"He said pretty much what Frank said."

"So, there you have it. Ghost in My Heart is ready to rock!" Marty burns through an early-eighties thrasher riff, something vaguely Metallica or Anthrax.

The plan was to form a band in cool-as-shit Prague, dominate the local scene, then blow back into the American market. Forty-two, Marty is, for a rocker, no electric chicken, but he is also, as the young girls say, some visibly mortified upon learning his age while still under the sheets, well preserved, and every inch a lead singer and guitarist, every inch a rock star. He wears eye make-up and pulls it off, kind of.

The son of the great Melissa Rayburn, film star and, over the past two decades, director of popular romantic comedies, Marty Rayburn does not know, exactly, who fathered him, though once, a bit tipsy at a party she was throwing at her home in Beverly Hills, his radiant mother hinted that Marty had been the issue of a tryst with Jim Morrison. The math worked, but by 1970 Morrison was puffy and spiraling. Melissa was the hottest prospect in Hollywood. The Doors finished their final album, *L.A. Woman,* in the fall of 1970. Melissa's little rocker rolled out on August 13.

"Let's just say your pops was a rider on the storm," his mother said inscrutably, sloshing her martini, and would not say another word on the subject. It was '93. Marty's first non-garage band had bombed at the Whisky, squandering their big break. Marty would graduate from Loyola Marymount, at the age of twenty-seven, with a 2.7 GPA and a degree in creative writing. He would form his next band that summer.

Bad Santa rocked the L.A. club scene through '98, had a less than triumphant though not disastrous stint at the Whiskey, and hit the road for five solid years, trying to build a fan base that proved quicksilver, selling CDs spottily, but never breaking through. When the movie by the same name as the band became a hit in 2003, Bad Santa became a joke. A music critic for the *De Moines Register* quipped that Bad Santa was really bad Santana though they only had one song, arguably two, that referenced Carlos Santana by any musical measure, and that Billy Bob Thornton's reprisal of the role had tighter comedic rhythm than Marty and chums had musical. It was a gratuitous, wholly inappropriate linkage, but the other four band members saw the proverbial writing on the wall of Marty's dream of stardom, and split.

"So who's played at the . . . ?" Melissa Rayburn asks her son, but can't duplicate the Czech pronunciation.

"The Palác Akropolis. Only the Pixies, the Strokes, Kid Loco and the Dead Kennedys, to name a few."

"Who you opening for?"

"Who said we're opening?"

"Who you opening for?"

She reads his fucking mind. "A Slovak rap-slasher band called Metafuck. Can you put ten grand in my account?"

"How's Red?"

"He died, Mom."

"What of? He was only seven."

"Boxers don't live long. He got sick about nine days ago and I had him put down." Melissa had been fond of the animal. "So, you'll transfer the money into my account?"

"Why can't you live on your trust? Just about any single guy could live on seven grand a month. You're not doing drugs again?"

"No. Fuck no. Betty Ford's gentle minions healed me."

"No one's ever healed. You know that. You'll always be recovering, until you start using again."

"I'm way past that shit. I don't even want it. I'm not even tempted. Pussy's my drug."

"Fine way to talk to your mama," she chuckles. "Yeah, I'll plunk ten grand into your account. But tell me what you need it for."

"Equipment," he lies. He's paying his band out of his own pocket.

"Did you watch that rough cut I sent you yet?"

"Yeah, it's okay. In the wheelhouse of your formula, but somehow fresh."

"What would you call it?" He's been titling his mother's movies for more than a decade.

"Call it *Kiss Him Off.*"

"Racy," she almost hisses.

"But double-edged." He wants to get off the phone. Skimming from her many millions has gotten to be such a chore.

"I like it," she says.

He gathers all of Red's toys and other doggy paraphernalia into a black garbage bag and hauls it to a trash bin flanked by recycling bins. He should separate the plastics, at least, but doesn't. Reentering his apartment, he is overwhelmed by the animal's odor even though his cleaning woman has scrubbed the place down twice since Red was euthanized.

His apartment, by Euro standards, is a large two bedroom; the smaller bedroom he's padded and turned into a practice space. He's in the middle of writing a new song, a soulful rock ballad whose working title is "One-Night Stand." He's satisfied with the chorus:

You're just a one-night stand
For a dude in a band
Just one stop along the road,
Just a one-night stand
For a guitar-playin' man
Gotta get back, get back to the show.

Pretty harsh, but he'll soften it in the verses, suggest that the "guitar-playin' man" has finally found his soul mate but is contractually obligated to remain on the road. Something like that. He'll work on the bridge tonight when he gets back home. He and Frank are going to check out a Czech chick singer at the *Café Na půl cesty* in Pankrác.

Frank has been his wingman since Bad Santa went down in flames. A terrific lead guitarist who played with some of the better bands in San Diego and L.A., and who'd actually made a living as a sessions player for a number of years, Frank moved to Prague fourteen months ahead of Marty. He chased a woman who OD'd eight months after his arrival. He'd have followed her into oblivion had Marty not arrived. Marty has been supporting him ever since. They don't talk about money. Marty just pays for everything and pays each band member thirty thousand crowns, a little over fifteen hundred a month. He also pays Frank's rent in addition to the thirty thousand crowns.

Marty wears tight leather pants that feature his eye-catching package, a white diaphanous peasant shirt, and black steel toe boots. He wears a leather band around his right wrist, a diamond-studded Rolex on his left. His brass belt buckle says "Harley," though he's never clamped his thighs around one. His naturally curly brown hair cascades past his shoulders. He is clean-shaven. The cobra tattooed on his neck peeks over his shirt collar.

Frank is in despair. He came to Prague to reconnect with his baby sister,

Helena, who had wanted to be dead between the ages of eleven and seventeen, but had been quite healthy for more than fifteen years. She fled to Prague because their grandparents are Czech, their mother was Czech, and they both spoke Czech through their childhoods in Sacramento, then L.A. The months before her death, Helena worked in their grandparents' flower shop, continued to write poetry that got published in some of the more prestigious literary journals in America, and was absorbed into Prague's nightlife. Because he didn't go out with her that night, Frank doesn't know what she OD'd on, though he knows it wasn't heroin or cocaine. As far as he could gather, it was an accident. She took the same shit everyone in her group took that night, something like Ecstasy but not, and she collapsed on the dance floor. Marty thinks he saved Frank from a similar fate and Frank doesn't even bother to set the record straight. Marty is a self-aggrandizing, narcissistic asshole, a self-deluded rich boy with visions of grandeur. Frank hated him the moment they met, but nonetheless hooked his wagon to Marty's phony though moneyed star.

Frank does not like being Marty's guitar whore. He is two or three light years beyond Marty in terms of musicianship, and has no delusions as to what will come of fucking Ghost in My Heart. Aging rockers continue to rock only if there is a substantial audience that recalls them in their youths. Marty's five years on the road garnered him a "fan base" about the size of most folks' Facebook accounts, a couple thousand email addresses many of which are dead. The band wasn't bad; Marty was a good front man, or, he'd have been a good one in the '80s. He was and is an anachronism.

But Frank will put his head down and play Marty's ridiculous songs, see the whole situation for what it is, a job. Marty's the boss, and Frank will placate him for humble remuneration.

When will all this end? What will Frank do for the rest of his life?

He meets Marty at the entrance to the Pankrac metro. He does not roll his eyes at Marty's costume. He is used to this look, and is beyond being embarrassed walking into clubs with him. He lights a cigarette and bumps shoulders with Marty.

As they stroll towards the club, Marty chatters about strategy, how Ghost in My Heart is going to dominate the local club scene, then tour Central Europe, and then get into some of the mid-range summer music festivals. There's an English-speaking agent Marty wants Frank to meet. The guy's had successes, and is going to catch their set at Palác Akropolis. Blah, blah, blah. Frank halts, slowly crushes his butt with his boot toe. He has reached a limit, hit a wall, been filled up past his eyebrows with Marty's bullshit.

"What's up, dude?" Marty is smiling but wrinkling his brow.

"Do you have any idea how ridiculous you sound?"

Marty makes a stuttering whisper; his mouth is open. The sound is issuing from the back of his throat. He is still smiling, though the furrows in his brow deepen.

"Name me one motherfucking band that got its start in Central Europe. And don't say the Beatles in Hamburg. They don't count."

"Why not?" Marty asks weakly.

"Jesus Christ." Frank lights another cigarette. "Marty," he begins, in a tone one assumes when explaining to a child, "you're forty-two. I'm forty-four. We're playing music that was relevant twenty years ago, and we're playing it as such music was played twenty, thirty years ago. We're going nowhere. You're my cash cow, partner. I don't like you. I have never liked you. I find you fucking preposterous. But I must say that right this moment, for the first time, I feel something like compassion for you. Let's go to the club, listen to the chick, have a few drinks. Maybe something like a friendship can happen between us."

Frank commences walking. Marty flanks him, stunned silent.

Marty does not believe that Frank means what he just said. He thinks his friend has been under a lot of pressure, is still in mourning for the woman he followed to Prague. Marty will remain calm. "This band's pretty tight, Frank."

"Yeah, Marty, it's tight," Frank answers warily.

"I'm not stupid," Marty insists, his voice even. "What I think is that we're composing and performing classic rock that has an original flavor. Your guitar work is familiar yet incredibly unique."

"I rip off everyone from Chuck Berry to Alvin Lee, from Jeff Beck and Eric Clapton and Peter Townshend and Jimmy Page and Hendrix to goddamned Muddy Waters and Duane Allman and B.B. King. Oh, did I mention Eddie Van Halen? There's not an original bone in my body."

"You've synthesized all of those influences," Marty insists. A bum touches his forehead to the pavement in front of a KFC, his palms pressed together above his greasy hair in the traditional posture of an utterly fucked-up supplicant. Marty tosses a fifty-crown coin into his cup.

"Please don't do that."

"Do what?" Marty asks.

"Kiss my ass, stroke my ego, give me a verbal blow job. I don't need it. I don't want it."

"You know you're good."

"I'm technically damned good. I'm damned good at playing music I've hated for more than a decade. Let me amend that; I'm a musician and I hate music, most of the time. Minutes here and there I love the best of it, even, God help me, opera. But most of the time I hate it. Sometimes I hate anything that isn't silence, or the sound of a tram as it passes late at night, or the sound of tires through rain, or the sound of shoes on stairs, or the sound of a baby crying far enough away that I can sleep."

Two convivial plain Janes pass giggling; they're obviously goofing on something. Frank smiles; Marty understands nothing. "Those two chicks think you stuffed a wad of socks in your crotch."

Marty is unfazed. He grins. "The only thing I got stuffed in there is Megathing." Megathing is the name Marty gave his penis many years ago. He speaks of it as of a beloved younger brother.

"It doesn't fucking matter, Marty. People think that you stuff a wad of socks in your crotch. It's the cut of those leather pants, buddy." Frank is still smiling.

Marty chalks up Frank's comment to jealousy. He glances sideways at his lead guitarist. Why doesn't Frank use Grecian Formula? "Why don't you take care of that gray, son?"

"You're such a dick," Frank responds with no malice, as though he is not judging, just stating fact.

Marty wonders why Frank is alone. It's been months since that girl OD'd. "What was that girl's name, the one who OD'd? Was she a good fuck?"

Frank wheels around and smashes his fist into Marty's solar plexus. Then punches him in the throat. "She was my sister, you narcissistic piece of shit!"

Marty can't breathe. He falls to his knees, then onto his ass. His eyes are huge and his face is scarlet. Gurgling issues from his open mouth. His breath comes back in tiny spurts that ratchet up to gasps, then panting. He holds his throat with one hand, his chest with the other. "Your sister?" he finally rasps.

They are playing Marty's "Thunder Woman" before two hundred or so blistered souls at Palác Akropolis but no one gives a shit. They are loud, the song is melodious in a Bon Jovi, rock ballad kind of way, and most of the crowd is engaged. As Frank kicks into his solo, he finds the eyes of an incredibly beautiful fifteen-, sixteen-, or seventeen-year-old girl. She is blond, tall, and buxom. She is standing in a clutch of other lovely girls less radiant than she at the foot of the stage. She is wearing a halter top and short shorts. She has a large silver ring in the navel of her glorious, tight, tummy. When she was born, he was at the top of his game in L.A., making good money doing sessions. His guitar work is on scores of albums, CDs by some of the heavy hitters of the '90s. Helena, a real artist, had found her voice and was a young star in the poetry world, which she joked was rather like being a world-class field hockey goalie.

Helena neither approved nor disapproved of Frank's whoring during those years. Chicks swarmed his brooding, slim good looks. Once in a while, he'd introduce a girlfriend, a woman he found interesting enough to spend a few weeks hanging with, to his sister. Helena was always polite, decent, nonjudgmental.

But after their mother's death, all they'd had was one another. He raised her, or, they raised each other. They spoke their broken Czech sometimes for privacy's sake. He witnessed her become a true artist; he didn't understand much of what she wrote; he wasn't at all trained in the art of poetry, but he knew that what she wrote was authentic, somehow, haunted by a dogged necessity. Her art was not a matter of choice.

That radiant child is giving him sexual energy as he squeals through the heart of his solo; he's disgusted by her come-hither stare, but cannot take his eyes off of hers. He wants to go to her, put a fatherly arm around her shoulder, and tell her to stay the fuck away from musicians.

Empire

1994

Babičko:

I know that you will not understand this, and Mom and Dad will not translate it for you. I wanted to wait until you yourself were gone, but I can't wait any longer. I'm weary, but very calm, and have no reason to continue; not even you, whom I love more than anyone but can barely talk to, are reason enough. We pantomime a lot, you and I, and you stroke my hair and hug me a lot, and I stutter through my bit of Czech and smattering of German, but it is perhaps precisely because we speak so little that what we communicate is so basic and uncluttered, so fundamentally true.

Babi, I have found the perfect place from which to leave the earth. As we tramped around, John didn't know that I was searching for such a place. When I found it I sent him away.

When you visited the family in Vancouver, I was so small, and so mystified to hear you speak Czech with Mom and Dad. They never spoke it in front of me when you were not there, though I heard it in hushed tones from their bedroom all my childhood. Only your all-too-infrequent presence over the years brought it out of their bedroom into my life. I loved to hear its music. God, it is so beautiful, and learning what little I have, since visiting you last summer and this one that is passing, has been wonderful. I will never have the grammar. How do children learn those endings? Different prepositions for different cases? That damned little 'r' with a hook over it, whose idea was such a sound as that, not to mention the long and short vowels that really do make talking sound like singing? When I try to speak you are so patient, Babi, and when I get frustrated you just give me more food and smile!

You told me once that you visited Tirol when you were young, before the war. The River Inn is narrow and pushes quickly through Innsbruck. I'll never understand the mechanics of rivers, how their sources remain constant. I'm sure it's very simple and all I'd have to do is check an encyclopedia, but I'd rather on some scores remain mystified. Certainly in the case of rivers such willful ignorance makes watching them more intriguing. The currents of the Inn are swift and swirling.

I'd thought perhaps Venice would be the proper point of entry to Nothingness, but the place has, despite its decadence and pretensions, a sense of humor. It's too easy to laugh in Venice, to weep in Munich and Vienna, to grow angry in Paris, to sigh in Rome. And of course I could never leave my life in Prague, for there it is too easy, in an understated Czech way, to love.

No, this little city of Innsbruck is perfect; its swirling, hustling river is perfect. After sending my bemused husband away, I tried to figure out what makes this place perfect to die in, besides the river. I'll try to explain, but first I need to tell you that despite what Mom and Dad say, I'm not going to "beat this thing." It's only going to get worse, until I'm too weak to determine when and where. If I had lived a long life like you, I would likely be inclined to "let nature take its course"; but you must know that it is different for the young. John drones about the wonders of modern science, but I know there will be no wonder cure for me. I have chosen the hour and manner of my passing, snatched the initiative from nature. Babi, my dear Babička, my sweet, stooped joyous and wise Czech grandmother, I cannot tell you how liberating such a choice feels. I am full of my own life, I am myself to the brim of being, and if there is a god, it either sanctions my death or remains wholly, even passionately indifferent. I am filled with a power only the living dead may possess, and I joined the ranks of such the moment I decided, determined with everything I am, to leave existence on my own terms.

When the denial of death is cast off one becomes a puny saint of sorts. At least I may judge and speak from this moment until my self-appointed passing without inhibition and with absolute impunity. I may speak as the river moves, with a frankness beyond reckoning, beyond all lies, both the beautiful kind and the kind that are evil.

The distinction is important to understanding why this little Tyrolean city is perfect for death. Babičko, it has no soul. Every city, every little village or burg, every tiny cluster of humanity acquires an essence beyond its constituents. To me, this is a soul, a collective identity that, for better or worse, resonates, like a tuning fork, through the hearts of those who identify with a place. There is no such resonance here. There is hollow, folkish pride, I suppose. Some men actually wear those ridiculous Tyrolean hats whose green felt is dotted with tiny shiny medals signifying, I suppose, memorable mountain hikes. Some of the hats have pheasant feathers arcing from them, and I recall a woman anthropologist once told me a man's feathers are a serious matter. In some "primitive" tribes, otherwise brave warriors will run for cover at a sprinkling of rain, fearing the wilting of their war feathers. These Tyrolean Austrians no doubt similarly associate erect feathers with virility, but, God, they do look silly! And if they are concerned with the mechanics of their own procreative prowess, there is no discernible passion in them, and not a speck of joy. Perhaps I am projecting onto these good people, Babi, perhaps I am being terribly unfair to come to their city, walk around a little, and proclaim them to be without a civic soul. But I have never, anywhere, felt such a lack of life in the living as in this gorgeous, pristine little city cradled by the Alps.

I'd love to ask you what you thought about it when you visited before the war, but even if you were here I could not ask such a question. Oh, I could ask, *Jak bylo Innsbruck kdy ty tady taky byla?* And you would puzzle a moment but then get my gist, and answer, *Hezky, velmi hezky*. Though of course you would have the proper endings, but beyond noting its prettiness—and it is quintessentially pretty, not beautiful, for beauty requires profound flaws in essential symmetries—you would not be able to tell me of the presence or absence of *duch*. It is so powerfully odd to be someplace so pretty and effervescent and not feel an essence, that is, to feel an absence.

The whole country is odd, Babi. Historically, they're Germans and not Germans. They were occupied by the Nazis, and were themselves the most passionate anti-Semites.

I was in a pub in the Old Town the other day, a few hours after seeing John off to Munich where he thinks I'll join him after a week of "getting my head straight" here in Yodelsburg. There was a table of American students mixed with English-speaking local students and a young Austrian professor. They were chattering in English, and when the young professor heard me order a beer and double shot of schnapps in wretched German he struck up a polite conversation, and invited me to join the group. He stated in a non-patronizing tone that he admired a healthy-looking woman who could place such an order so early in the day. The group was deep in congenial debate regarding a lecture they'd attended the previous evening. An American expatriate writer spoke about being a Jew in Vienna for twenty years. One young woman said it was "ghastly" that her summer school abroad program had invited someone to talk on such a sensitive subject. Weren't they being bad guests? Didn't residents of this clean, pretty little city deserve not to be embarrassed in such a fashion?

"Are there many former Nazis here?" I asked offhandedly, and the table hushed a moment.

"It's a very complicated matter," the young professor said. He was a small, thin-faced, fair-haired smilingly earnest person. "A lot of these old guys walking their dogs on the promenade along the river must have served as Nazis. Most of the Death Camps were run by men from this part of Austria, men like Stragl at Treblinka."

The boyish professor launched into a calm and measured lecture. He spoke of the antipathy between the Social Democrats and the Christian Socials before the "Nazi occupation," how Dollfus, a fascist of sorts himself, rejected National Socialism on the basis of the historical bond between Christian and German culture, and that the Nazis had substituted the former with Teutonic paganism and perverted the latter with racism. It seems this Dollfus fellow saw Austrians as the better Germans. Well, he got rid of the Social Democrats rather bloodily, and the Austrian Nazis eventually got rid of him in similar fashion, and presto, on March 15, 1938 the Nazis were wooing two-hundred thousand Viennese on the Heldenplatz. The wonder boy speculated that the Reich became a psychological substitute for the 1918 loss of empire. Indeed, by 1942, there were more than six hundred thousand official Nazis in this little country, this tiny wedge of the Habsburg sprawl, a representation proportionally larger than in Germany itself.

"But you must understand that very few Austrians anticipated either the war or the Final Solution. Neither did the rest of the world. In 1938, Hitler was controversial, but generally respected internationally."

"Do you hate Jews?" I asked him, and he was clearly taken aback. The sprightly coed, probably from Georgia, who had considered it bad manners to invite a Jew to lecture about being a Jew, stared at me with her mouth open.

"Of course I do not hate Jews," the fellow answered calmly and with persuasive dignity.

"Do you believe the old men who walk their dogs on the promenade along the river hate Jews?"

"I cannot speak for them," he answered, "but it is possible that some do, in the same sense that old men walking dogs along promenades in your own country may harbor such sentiments."

Of course he was right, and I told him so. Then I related my observation that the small city of Innsbruck has no soul, and to my mild astonishment he comprehended my sense.

"Yes, perhaps something is missing, not just here but throughout the area."

"What can that be?" I pressed.

"In most of Germany, and even in Vienna, people have searched their consciences regarding collective guilt. Of course, many have rejected responsibility, but at least did so after first considering the prospect. At least they forced a choice upon themselves. I think that what you are sensing is a guilt so powerfully repressed it has become, to use a popular figure from astrophysics, a collapsed star in the heart, a black hole." Then, after a pause, he said, "You know, an old synagogue will be rebuilt not far from here. Perhaps that will help."

He seemed a decent, even wise fellow, so I did not ask who would require the services of a synagogue, and the thought of a people for whom anti-Semitism is a defining cultural feature building ("rebuilding" he said) a synagogue where there are no Jews seemed an aesthetic corollary to the ubiquitous phenomenon of Jew-hating where there are no Jews. Perhaps, indeed, an empty synagogue will restore a soul to this city, allow the collapsed light in their hearts to bounce forth and reveal their passions, their true loathings and loves. The yodeling kitsch in shop windows, the men's feathered hats, the traditional necessity of jerking herds up forbidding slopes so they may shit some agrarian prosperity into lives made stern by topography, all that and the general tourist-driven prosperity of the place, the Mercedes's and clipped lawns and regimented gardens, the seeming ordinance against smiling in public—even more rigorously enforced it seems than in Slavic countries—and the river, pushing and swirling at thrice the pace of people's lives here, all of it assumes a grotesque sweetness in light of the prospect of their "rebuilding" a synagogue where there are no Jews. It is a lie one may celebrate, a lie of humane if silly compensation for evil lies.

So, perhaps it is not the case that the place is soulless, but that its soul is so shy it is quite beyond the comprehension of silence. To cease in the midst of such undeterminable essence, to will one's passing in the midst of such soul shyness, is not so much to die as to unborn oneself; as Jews will be unborn unto the Tyrolean synagogue, so I shall unborn myself unto this nervous little river.

It's hard to believe that a few hundred miles from here genocide is occurring again in earnest.

Babi, I must tell you the moment I freed myself to unbirth unto the River Inn. I was strolling the promenade along the right bank. It is quaintly narrow and shrub lined. There are nice benches every quarter kilometer or so.

It was early morning, five-thirty or so, not long after dawn, and John was still sleeping. We'd talked the night before about therapies, and John had been so typically upbeat and hopeful, and even I had been buoyed a little by his optimism, his foolish, sweet, so typically American optimism. That aspect of folks from the lower forty-eight is something even Canadians find mystifying. Anyway, I strolled the pretty promenade; the air was scrubbed and the river, the river moved at its unalterable rate of a seasoned runner doing six-minute miles. As I walked, I tried to assume John's optimism, to imagine a painless, ambulatory life into next summer, and the next and the next. And, Babi, I even imagined children! I crafted a fantasy in which I was cured, had a beautiful baby girl, and brought her to you in Prague! Babi, it was a beautiful waking dream, and my eyes misted and I grinned like an idiot.

But then I came upon a woman sitting on a bench facing the river. She was plainly dressed, clean and fairly well kempt. She had an alcoholic's rosy hue in her plump face, her face which remained, Babi, wholly expressionless, absolutely void of pain or terror or even sadness as she held her left hand palm down, thumb at the level of her solar plexus, and snapped a yellow Bic with her right hand directly under her down-turned palm.

Babi, I froze and stared for one, two, three seconds then ran past her a hundred meters then buckled over, sobbed convulsively. I dared not look back, and I heard nothing. No scream, no whimper, only the river and my own swallowed sobs. That silence, Babi, that lack of human sound laced with sibilant river and twittering birds and faint first traffic of morning, is that to which I commit my humanity. My humanity I give up, neither loving nor loathing the life of blessings and terrors I have traversed, to the chilling human mystery of that woman, who is this place which is a soullessness or shyness or both. And you, my mother's mother, my babička who will feed and comfort anyone or anything that happens upon the hearth, you who are a breast of small kindnesses unto life, I shall greet you in the River Inn.